NARAYANA

NARAYANA

TJ O'NEAL

TATE PUBLISHING
AND ENTERPRISES, LLC

Published by Tate Publishing & Enterprises, LLC
127 E. Trade Center Terrace | Mustang, Oklahoma 73064 USA
1.888.361.9473 | www.tatepublishing.com

Tate Publishing is committed to excellence in the publishing industry. The company reflects the philosophy established by the founders, based on Psalm 68:11,
"The Lord gave the word and great was the company of those who published it."

Book design copyright © 2014 by Tate Publishing, LLC. All rights reserved.
Cover design by Carlo nino Suico
Interior design by Jomel Pepito

Published in the United States of America

ISBN: 978-1-63122-799-8
1. Fiction / Science Fiction / General
2. Fiction / Science Fiction / Action & Adventure
14.05.02

A SECRET WORTH CREATING

Two feet alternated back and forth acting as pistons for the torso above it. The torso was of a man who was clothed by a forest-green suit and decorated with several military medals. It was apparent to anyone who saw him that he was an officer and possibly a war hero. His face was aged, but the hair upon his head was fine and still able to retain a brown shade. The prestigious look gave him the perfect amount of swagger as he walked steadily alone through an empty and dull-lighted hallway. At the end of the hallway was a room separated by two stainless doors. As the officer approached the doors, they horizontally slid open revealing the room's interior. Its back was covered by a large window while a maple desk with a leather chair overlapped the view. Seeing that these features seemed to be the only noticeable aspects of the room, he deemed the room bland and tasteless. However, his interest was not in the room. Looking harder, he found the top of a head partially exposed over the chair's backing. Target in sight, the officer now stood just past the entrance of the door with his spine straight and his hat tucked underneath his right armpit.

"Dr. Nar Porter," he declared with an assuming tone.

Behind the chair sat a man in a black suit. The voice had drawn his attention away from the skyline view of the city below. He turned his head just slightly over his shoulder as if he wanted to hear more. His head returned to its original view and he stood.

His body remained facing the glass window; his eyes still fixed on the city.

"Colonel Goodwin," Porter responded with his back facing the well-decorated officer.

"It has been a while."

"Yes it has."

"I hope all is well." Goodwin's tone seemed insincere.

"It is as good as it can be," Porter replied with a minor implication.

Colonel Goodwin sensed the slight hostility Porter had in his voice and noticed him lift his hand towards his mouth. The hand held a glass that had been gingerly filled with a brownish-gold liquid. Goodwin assumed it was liquor due to Porter's delicate consumption. Porter swallowed and returned the glass to his side.

Goodwin spoke again. "You cannot drink away your wretchedness."

Porter looked over his shoulder again. "You act as though you feel for me. We both know you don't, so please enlighten me on what you need."

"I was hoping I could talk to you about an opportunity."

"An opportunity?" Porter snapped back. "Why would I feel the need to do business with you?"

"Listen, I know what you have been working on."

Porter laughed with subtlety. "So you have someone spying on me? Now, why would you want to do that? Am I posing a threat to national security?"

"Not exactly, if anything, the opposite. I need your help and I believe we could help each other."

Porter turned completely around and faced Goodwin directly. His tie hung loose around his neck with the top button undone. Despite his relaxed look, Porter's young face seemed to be tired and worn out.

"How could you possibly help me, Colonel?" Porter asked. "I have already lost everything."

"Not everything. We have discovered something. A planet."

"A planet? This is your offer?" Porter blurted in confusion. "How is this supposed to help me?"

"I am gathering together a crew for a secret space expedition." Goodwin paused. "I need something that only you could accomplish."

Porter began to grow slightly irritated as he set his glass down with authority. Being that Porter was of average build, he avoided flaunting a physical threat like an enraged animal. Instead, he initiated a continuous glare into the colonel's eyes attempting to play mind games. This tactic worked and the full truth was drawn out.

"I want the virus," Goodwin admitted.

"Well, it isn't for sale, Colonel."

Goodwin began his sales pitch. "For the right price it is. I know what it is that you truly want, and I believe we have similar interests." Porter's attentiveness became so seemingly obvious that a child would have noticed. "We both want the same thing— life. I am giving you the opportunity to create just like you want, completely funded by the government."

Porter knew in his mind this was exactly what he was interested in. He knew that this opportunity was how he could show his proof. However, he did not want Goodwin to know it directly. He thought of ways in which he could show his interest and not seem overzealous. Figuring out the perfect reaction Porter responded. "What if I say no?"

"Then the best of luck to you." Goodwin attempted to initiate the game of poker. "We both know that you will never achieve it without my funding."

"And we both know there is always more. Something that is worth hiding deep within the fine print."

Goodwin smiled.

"I need a weapon, something I can use. After all, this mission isn't exactly for discovery."

THE FATE OF AN OPPORTUNITY

Christian Philips looked down to the city in which he lived as he watched people and cars move like ants and toys. The Philips's apartment was recognized by friends and family as being substantial in height, but it seemed to have good reason. Philips enjoyed the view from the bedroom balcony in which he found himself now. It was relaxing to allow the gentle wind brush his face like a kiss from the sky. Though his balcony was a simple pleasure, it always offered him the same beautiful view of a starry nighttime sky. To him, it was a great place to think of the world's growth and its potential.

The world as Christian Phillips knew it was relatively simple and to the point. He thought he had it figured out complete being that twenty-eight years of life gives someone the perfect amount of experience. The year was now 2106 and people still dressed in popular clothing, cars still drove with four wheels, and entertainment was still overvalued. The architecture of cities had changed for the better in the sense that buildings had become more energy efficient and structurally advanced. Also, devices had become more adaptable, technology was smarter, and almost everything had a sleek and clean appearance.

However, from what he knew, the world had developed but had not significantly changed from what it had been in the prior century. There had been no invention or innovation that had truly altered the way people view life. Humans appeared as though they were stuck in a phase of upgrading in which there was only the desire to improve what had already existed. Philips wanted humanity to discover more ideas and explore more capacities. He desired the thrill of exploration and the excitement of human discovery. One could say he was relatively an ambitious individual. Lacking in explorative ecstasy, he felt it necessary to accept any opportunity that could possibly offer this characteristic. It just so happened that his first offer at the opportunity was from the air force colonel, John Goodwin.

During their first encounter two months ago, Goodwin seemed as though he were a stern man who always got his way. However, when the idea of space exploration was pitched in Philips's direction, thinking was nearly absence. Philips unquestionably accepted the offer to travel to an untouched planet. When Philips had lost his arm in combat, he was left with somewhat of an early retirement and a driving desire for further adventure. Being that he had been one of the army's best field engineers in his service time, Goodwin felt it necessary to feed that desire. With the contract signed, Philips was assured to be a part of the *New Sumeria* crew.

Philips found himself preparing for the next day launch by thinking on his balcony. He shifted his eyes from the city to the stars above him repeatedly as though he were comparing the two. It was obvious that the expedition would be a long journey into space; however, he was unsure of how long he would be away from the only world he knew. He imagined traveling in a space ship for years at a time in dark, open space. He thought long and hard about the continuous stagnation that came with space travel, but he was able to redirect his thinking toward its reward. There was the possibility of a new path and story for the human race. A unique and new planet that would not only be appeasing to the eye but also offer advanced progress for humanity or even a new beginning. The possibilities at this point seemed endless.

Christian's train of thought was effaced as he felt his back tingled by a familiar touch. As the sensation spread throughout his back, he turned slightly to discover two delicate and milky hands caressing his shoulders. The hands belonged to his young wife, Alicia. He turned away from his musing and let her presence draw his complete attention. She began to move her hand to the back of his head and tenderly stroked his light, short hair. Philips responded as he finger combed the blonde hair from her forehead and ran his hand down its length. Their skin met with a kiss despite the enlarged stomach that came between them. Philips then bent down to the middle of her small body and kissed her clothed stomach gently and stood up and met her eyes once more.

"I already miss you two," said Philips, addressing Alicia and her tummy.

"I wish you could be here for when it happens," Alicia responded.

"I will be. In a way. I will see it from space."

"It just isn't the same, but I guess it is better than if you didn't see your baby boy at all."

Philips paused for a moment and continued, "Nothing matters more to me than to see you two on that day. Alicia, I will return soon. It won't be too long of a trip."

She chuckled a little.

"Well, I'd rather see you return in one piece after a long time than see you not return at all."

The comment gave Philips a dark feeling that he chose to suppress. Philips could see through Alicia's smiles and distinguish her true feelings. He knew that she was not entirely fond of her husband leaving for a space expedition prior to the birthing of their child. Nevertheless, she always supported Philips no matter what and was willing to invest a lot of time and emotion towards his passions.

"Don't worry about me babe, I will be fine. I will be there and back in no time. And I will have been one of ten people who have brought remarkable discoveries and developments to mankind."

"I know you will," Alicia replied. "And you will have a son to return to that will be so proud of his father."

Alicia reached into her pocket and pulled out a blue, beaded necklace. Attached to the end of the beads was a small, round-edged cross that was made from wood. The wood had been stained giving a glossy, light-brown finish. She delicately held it in her hand. She paused for a moment staring at the cross and smiled at its polished glow. Her hand reached above her head and toward the head of her husband. The rosary found its way over the top of his head and around his neck. It rested upon his muscular shoulders and the cross upon his lean chest, between his dog tags and his heart. For the moment, he wore it to please Alicia, but his life had removed any significance the cross carried.

Alicia looked into his eyes once more.

"Chris, I want you to have this cross. It was once mine, but I think you could use it more than me. Use it to give you guidance and faith when you are up there."

"Thanks, Alicia. I will."

"I love you."

"I love you, too."

The two kissed again as Philips held her face softly with both hands. He then took his hands and placed them on the top of Alicia's rounded stomach. While looking down at his child, he had a subtle and abysmal feeling of not returning. He quickly tried to shake the feeling by looking at his wife's face. She smiled at him once again and suddenly he felt the thought melt away to the point that he became lost in her elegant light skin and sea blue eyes.

MORE THAN A SHIP?

Philips's final night with his wife was a blur. He had full intentions on making their last good-bye before the launch a long drawn out process. In actuality, it seemed brief because of the distraction the expedition created in his mind. Philips could not devote himself completely and regretted it as he was driven to the launch site. The vehicle had tinted windows in the interior and outside preventing sight from both. Also, there was a tinted window separating the driver from Philips in the back seat. Essentially, he had been barred from any knowledge of the enigmatic destination. The mission was a secret mission, but he slightly questioned why. He thought a momentous event, such as this launch, would be viewed on every television worldwide. Instead, he was just as blind to the mission as anyone else. The fact was he had no idea where he was being taken and why the mission was secret.

When the vehicle came to a stop, Philips was not entirely sure if they had arrived. He was soon answered as his side door opened and a man gestured for his exit. Philips grabbed his bag and gradually exited the vehicle. He scanned the man with his eyes, having not done so previously, and faintly appreciated the appearance and wardrobe that was before him. The man was a light skinned, bald man who wore a pair of dark sunglasses and a dark suit. His attire was relatively appropriate for the somewhat kidnapping Philips had just experienced. Yet, Philips was unfazed by this probable concept.

Alternatively, the launch site was a remote area that only a handful of people could have known about. Its land was hot, dry, and had an orange covering. Dirt and dust kicked around in the wind as though it a part of the air. Above the desert's lifeless appeal was a blank, blue sky that did not possess a single cloud. However, something else was grabbing his attention at the moment. Before him was a great, metal frame that must have been the equivalent of several buildings put together; it was an entirely white machine with letters written in black and gold. The letters spelled words that read *New Sumeria*. At this point it was ambition that had brought Philips to the space adventure, but it was grace, sophistication, and innovation that had drawn him toward the spacecraft. Phillips found himself gazing at one of most astonishing piece of technology he had ever envisioned. He was in shock at first as he walked slowly in his army fatigues with a bag in his hand. It was so advanced, in his eyes, that even in his wildest imagination he could not fathom this idea. He had been under the impression that the technology in the everyday life was the farthest human modernization had come. In no way did he think that there was machinery that was this progressive.

Examining it further, he noticed it had a glass front that resembled what he thought was a potential face. Underneath, it was prompted by three bended leg-like structures with one in the front and two stationed side-by-side in the back. Around its core were what looked like two full circular tracks that were parallel. The two tracks both had individual thrusters that resided on the bottom part of the ship. To Philips, it seemed as though the thrusters were intended to rotate around the ship so that they could be used on its top and bottom. The same idea was present upon the backside of the ship. Encompassing the area was a semi-circular track with a thruster as well.

Finally, Philips reached the ship's entrance and had to climb an elevated slope that was extracted from the ship. As he walked up the slope, he noticed Colonel Goodwin greeting each crew member that came aboard. Somehow Philips was able to sneak past the colonel without his attention being attracted. Now abroad the ship, he became captured by it once more. His head was on a swivel while his eyes took pictures with every blink. The bay of the ship was an area about the size of two basketball courts that held several parked vehicles. The vehicles were a mixed batch of ground and air usage. The ground vehicles looked like enclosed dune buggies that had been specialized for rough terrain while the air vehicles were more sophisticated with what looked to be gravitational lifts upon each wing.

A loud clanking of machinery and a piercing hiss sound drew Philips's eyes to the slope. With a series of folding motions, the extracted slope retracted itself into the ship. The slope became a wall of the ship that separated him and the dry topography. The orange scenery would be the last part of Earth Phillips would be in contact with. They were now completely shut-off from the only world they had known and expected to move forward. Philips had one last picture of Earth in his mind. Attempting to think back to its image, he could not recall anything other than mounds and wind of orange. It was like staring into the sun; the image had been present despite its removal.

It was a lot for Philips to take in and he desired a break. The sudden changes had temporarily overwhelmed him. Needing to experience something familiar, Philips decided to initiate his detective skills. He had always had a lot of questions so naturally he developed an investigative personality. Though it typically amused him, it tended to make him slightly over proactive. The skill consumed a lot of his time; however, he thought it might be beneficial during the trip.

Like a light switch, his natural talent seemed to just flick on as he found himself looking in the direction of Goodwin. Goodwin had entered the bay of the ship with the rest of the crew. Philips watched Goodwin engage in a conversation with a man of average build and bland clothing. He had a hunch that he was some type of scientist based off of the lack of stylishness in his glasses. The scientist fiddled with the pair briefly until they were fully adjusted. His hair was dark and unkempt and his starry eyed look showed that he was intrigued by most things. By watching and eavesdropping while the two conversed, Philips was able to gather some information.

"Dr. Thatcher, it so good to have you aboard." Goodwin smiled. "It is great to have someone of your wit on my vessel."

Thatcher returned a smile and spoke. "Thank you, Colonel. It is an honor to be on this amazing space craft. I have never seen anything like this before."

"Ah, there are some things the United States government keeps a secret my friend," Goodwin said as he chuckled.

"Well, let's not hope there are too many secrets during this trip."

Thatcher's joke was dry humored; yet, Goodwin ignored it as a remembrance cued.

"…I truly enjoyed your latest book," said Goodwin, diverting the topic.

"Thank you very much, Colonel. You know not a lot of people can't appreciate and fully understand the work I do in physics. Many believe it is just a job where people can make up theories of whatever they want and act as though they are smarter than everyone else. They don't understand that science is a gradual process."

"Well that's a shame for those people then. I do enjoy your work Dr. Thatcher and that is why you are aboard my ship."

Philips was attempting to hold back a laugh as the dramatic irony of the conversation was almost too much to bear. It did not take a conscious effort to know that Goodwin was playing politician. Goodwin was typically a successful raconteur and could win over the hearts of whomever he talked to. In fact, he most likely had a possible career as a politician in line for him following this expedition. His persona met the job qualification seeing that he had perfected the ability to stand in front of people and hold a fake personality. It would not have been extremely surprising for Philips to discover that the expedition was actually for malpractice of some sort. If it was not for the concept of space travel and discovery, then Philips might have thought more of Goodwin's intentions.

The conversation concluded and Philips watched Goodwin matriculate around greeting people one at a time. A few people experienced his schmoozing before Goodwin made eye contact with him. Philips watched him as he walked with incredible posture in his officer's attire. His attire came with a look of determination and his face expressed experience. With confidence in each step, he lessened the distance between them. He now stood face to face with Philips and the two exchanged a hand shake.

Addressing Philips by his rank, Goodwin started the interaction, "I am glad you were able to join us Lieutenant Philips."

"Would not miss it for the world, sir!" Philips cracked.

"Walk with me," Goodwin said as he held his arm out with his palm up to signal the way. The two began to walk into the ship's deep interior while Goodwin continued. "It is nice to be able to talk to a person such as yourself. Someone who I can relate to. Someone who can fight in combat yet someone who you can have a civil and intelligent conversation with." He subtly pointed in the direction behind them with his thumb. "See the other crew members possess only one of those characteristics. But, they are good at what they do, so that is why they are here." Philips nodded in agreement. "So what do you think of my ship?"

"It is very impressive sir. I had no idea we possessed this kind of equipment."

Goodwin snickered a little and put his arm around Philips.

"Come on Philips," he said playfully. "It is the twenty-second century."

Philips displayed a quick smile. "I guess so."

Philips felt a sense of uneasiness in the midst of this conversation. His discomfort had been brought on by the recollection of the exchange between Goodwin and Thatcher. The mention of government secrets replayed through his mind. He began to think hard. Could Goodwin be hiding something that the crew is unaware of? What of it? Could it be something that is secret because it is detrimental?

"To be honest sir," Philips started again, "I am a little skeptical towards this mission. I mean after all it seems as though me and the rest of the crew are being left out of many things."

"Now why would I want my crew to be left out?" Goodwin smiled. "It is you all that are doing the research and grunt work for me. If anything, I am worried about you all not informing me."

"I guess I just wish I had a little more knowledge regarding this trip."

"Lieutenant, long story short, this is a mission of exploration. We are going to be discovering and potentially creating something new." He paused and recognized Philips's restless thought. "Are you alright Lieutenant?"

"Yes, yes, everything is fine." He paused. "It is just a lot to take in all in one sitting."

"Perfectly understandable. I'll tell you what; take some time to get acquainted with the ship. We will meet for debriefing following take off. But trust me, there is nothing that you should be concerned about. You, me, and the rest of the crew need each other. And it is essential that we work together, as crew members, so that we can impact and change the world."

"Thank you, sir."

The two parted and Philips walked a few halls until he found the room labeled with his name. He placed his bag on his bed and noticed ship standard shoes and uniform with his last name on it.

As he unfolded the uniform, he held it just before his face so that he could see its entire design. The material was spandex-like but slightly more lose fitting. Undressing from his fatigues was easy; on the other hand, getting into the uniform was more tasking as he struggled to force his head and limbs through the expanding material. On the contrary, it was comfortable. It seemed to keep him warm but not hot and it was almost tailored perfectly to his lean body type.

He now thought it appropriate to wander through the ship in order to learn its general make up and equipment. Promenading through the ship, he thought to himself that it had to have been designed by an alien race. The walls and ceilings were low in most parts but seemed rounded at the top. All the doors had lights in front of them that depicted whether the room was locked or not—green meant the door was unlocked while red meant the opposite. Each foot step Philips took echoed through the halls sounding as though someone were tapping on the side of aluminum can. The echoing was consistent through every hall but was not present when he would enter rooms and examine them. Every room seemed to have a large widescreen-like window that consumed a large part of a single wall. This design led Philips to the conclusion that he would eventually find himself standing in front of at least one of them. He knew that he would be engrossed in the interminable appearance of space and the potential atmospheric beauty of the new planet.

The minutes grew largely on Philips's watch as he realized how much of the ship he had covered. Conversely, he had not felt as though he had truly seen all of its remarkable competencies. To add on to his dissatisfaction, he had to face the intolerable truth that he was lost in its core. Lost for what, he thought as he circled in place looking for some sort of a directory. The time continued its labor on Philips's watch until he finally found a map description of the ship. He examined it long and hard and appreciated the fact that he had only viewed a small quadrant. He knew he would not be able to settle himself before the journey as long as there were undiscovered parts of the massive vessel.

Abruptly, Philips's probing was halted, for something new had attracted his attention. Behind him he heard the tapping of the aluminum can causing him to turn around. Walking towards him was a dark-skinned man wearing similar military fatigues in which he himself had arrived in. The man was muscular but was not massively built. His arms were forcing his sleeves to expand slightly, but they were not on the verge of ripping. Atop his head was a thick and short, dark Mohawk that faded into the side of his head. In his hand was a bag, similar to the one Philips arrived with, that was slung over his broad shoulders. He came close to Philips and stopped; they faced each other, eye to eye.

With a straight face he spoke. "Sergeant D.J. Watkins."

The two shook hands and Philips answered. "Lieutenant Christian Philips. Nice to meet you,"

"Army?"

"Yes, and you?"

"Marines, so I guess this means you aren't technically responsible for me."

"I don't think that pertains on this ship." Philips chuckled.

"If you insist." Watkins smiled. "What was your division?"

"I was in the 49th infantry. I was a combat engineer."

"No shit." Watkins paused. "I was a part of 4th and the 26th regiment. We fought with your infantry in a joint operation in Africa."

"Yes, I remember now." Philips grew saddened for a moment as he fiddled with the cross around his neck. "I try to forget though. We lost a lot of men there. I haven't been in combat since," he said as he rolled his sleeve up his arm holding out the palm side of his forearm. "Look's real doesn't it?"

"Prosthetic?"

"Yes."

"Everyone seemed to have lost a part of them in Africa."

Philips looked into Watkins's eyes and noticed a great deal of sorrow and regret. He knew there was a lot of pain that Watkins had chosen to bury deep within himself. Maybe a lost friend or family member. Maybe he feels the responsibilities that war can falsely place on an individual. Whatever the reason, Philips discerned that some aspects of a person should not be examined. Before he could jettison the topic, he watched Watkins, to his surprise, crack a forced smile through the pain.

"But that is the past and it leads us to the present," Watkins explained. "So maybe all this is a blessing. Listen man, I'm trying to find my room, so I am sure I will see you around. Oorah, my man." He patted Philips on the shoulder and walked away.

Automatically Philips recognized a sense of chemistry between him and Watkins. Despite the shortened interaction and the depressing memories brought about in their encounter, Philips could tell that Watkins had a cheerful and outgoing personality. His dialect was witty and quick and throughout their entire greeting Watkins displayed passion and emotion. He knew he would enjoy Watkins's company during the expedition.

Now that Watkins had left the vicinity, Philips turned back towards the directory and observed it once more. On the directory was something he had not noticed before. There were symbols for areas on the *New Sumeria* that were marked as restricted zones. Philips found these limitations to be rather confusing and suspicious considering the lack of restriction on areas such as the nuclear room. With a room name such as that, Philips felt as though the colonel might want to confine its access. He was quick to label it subtle irony, but curiosity began to consume him. *What was it about the word restricted that created so much hunger for answer?* He thought. Nevertheless, the question did not hinder his desire in the least bit as he found himself mobile once more.

Upon his mobilization, he had grown a large amount of enthusiasm, like a child waiting to open their presents on Christmas day. His excitement was fueled by the potential to find answers to this mysterious trip. Restricted, in the mind of Philips, was like an invitation to explore something further. Almost as though in every dictionary he had every perused through there was an absence of the word. Nonetheless, maybe, he thought, it was not his job to be a combat engineer on the ship but rather a detective for the other crew members. Yes, that was it. It was his responsibility to inspect every aspect of the ship and its mission so that he could report back to the crew. After all, he was assuming that each crew member was as ignorant of the mission as him.

Again his efforts at explanation were halted. His first reaction was frustration, but as he listened his feeling eased. He heard a voice but there was no one near him. A voice but not a human voice, for it was like something he had never heard before. It seemed to emanate from every side and corner of the ship. The voice was feminine and sophisticated but lacked a form of emotion in its tone. There was no affection, no sentiment, just solely informative.

"Welcome all crew members." It spoke. "Please at this time relieve yourselves of any belongs in your assigned rooms. In your rooms you should find your sanctioned flight uniforms. Please take the time to undress and redress in the uniform. Colonel Goodwin advises that all report to the cockpit of the ship for launch and debriefing at 0800. Thank you for your time and once more, welcome."

As the voice concluded, Philips checked his watch. Ten minutes to 0800 he read. He knew he had to postpone his investigative work once more. The thought was not incapacitating to Philips, for he knew the trip would give him more time to do so.

DEBRIEFING TO KEEP IT BRIEF

Having studied the ship directory thoroughly, Philips was able to commit every area on ship to his memory. Doing so allowed him to find the cockpit in which he stood. Surrounding him was the rest of the crew. Each crew member had taken what the voice had suggested and arrived in the cockpit with their uniforms and no belongings. Among those present, Philips recognized both Watkins and Thatcher. He thought, as the crew stood in relative proximity, that they resembled a sports team. They all looked the same and besides the colonel and two other mysterious men, they all expressed the same emotion. Astonishment was constant among the crew. The ship had not let up on its ability to amaze the crew members that were new to its charm. Inside was a set of unmanned pilot stations with holographic screens all around them. The theme throughout the cockpit seemed to be these screens. Philips watched as one of the mysterious men touched a set of the screens with his hand. He gracefully threw around the objects and the data on them simply by moving his arm and flicking his wrist. Philips became entertained with the man's antics. It was compelling to watch this man seem as though he were playing himself in a game. During his play, his slicked blonde hair shined from the light reflecting off his head. Though he was not of an athletic physique, his motions could have fooled someone into looking past his small frame. He spoke; however,

Philips was not entirely sure who it was towards. His words were intended for someone, but no one responded. This continued until he heard it. There it was again: the voice that he deemed as sophisticated and unemotional. It answered the man's requests and the two seemed to have a bantering relationship.

"Avi," said the man.

"Yes Mr. Dover," the feminine voice responded impassively.

"Check the pressure of the thrusters. Are they online?"

"Yes, it would seem as though power capability is a remarkable one-hundred percent."

"Well we wouldn't want to launch if it wasn't, now would we Avi?"

"It would seem so."

"Area clear for the launch?"

"It would seem that that is true as well."

He detected the attitude from the voice.

"Why, I programmed you to have a personality is beyond me."

The man now turned to Goodwin and spoke to him. It was brief but carried vital information as Goodwin informed the crew. "Please, everyone take a seat and buckle in before we begin travel."

Everyone acted like a flock of sheep walking in unison to the voice of their shepherd. The crew found a group of chairs that resided just behind the pilot stations and the holographic screens. Each seat came equipped with harnesses that attached from five points. Once the clicking of the center pieces concluded, Goodwin turned to the man operating the holographic screens and instructed him with a simple head nod. Both Goodwin and the man made their way to vacant chairs and constricted themselves to the harnesses as well. All the members were securely seated.

"Now Avi," the man ordered.

The voice began a count down from the number ten. Following the number one came a loud rumbling from the bottom of the ship and a violent shaking. Philips attempted to grab a stable object on his chair. His hands found a part of the armrests that he used as a handle to stabilize himself. Looking around he noticed everyone had already done the same. The ship sent a rush up from the sole of his boots to the top of his head. The force was so great that he was unable to move any muscle or ligament in his body. Although the sensation was brief and over after a few seconds, he had convinced himself it were a lifetime.

Despite the traumatic experience, it slipped his thoughts as the cockpit walls began to remove themselves. The walls shifted in sheets of metal, one at a time, until his entire surrounding was filled with darkness and a great blue mass below it. Upon the mass were streaks of scattered white and smaller masses of forest green. He looked beyond the blue and saw that the darkness was filled with dots of light and a giant, grey rock. A sense of relief settled over Philips as he admired the beauty of the Earth and its surroundings. He was relieved by the idea that the color orange would not be his only thought of Earth. The vivid portrait before him was much more than a color. In fact, its colors told a story. It was a story about Philips's past and future. The blue, green, and white were his past events while the darkness that surrounded was his future. He was blind to his future, veiling his subtle fear of the unknown. However, he hoped to possibly brighten the darkness and wanted to do so with more knowledge and discovery.

"Welcome to space," Goodwin began. "Enjoy this view now because it will be gone in a moments."

Goodwin's comment proved to be true as a similar sensation forced Philips and the rest of the crew members' heads to the back of their seats. Philips watching the visual from the cockpit windows fade to complete darkness and lighted dots. Unlike before, the force did not stop completely but instead weakened gradually. Eventually, it seemed as though the force had become nonexistent as he watched Goodwin and the mysterious man stand from their chairs. Goodwin made his way to the front of the crew, facing the group, while the other man went back to his playing screens.

There Goodwin stood before the crew with the same uniform as every other individual aboard. Even though he was stripped of his military medals and tailored symbol of power, he still personified leadership. No matter what he wore, he possessed a vibe of power and authority. Simply his presence in front of the crew was able to draw each of the crew member's attention. He held his hands behind his back and stood with a perfect posture of one-hundred eighty degrees.

The colonel began to speak trading eye contact with each seated crew member.

"This is *New Sumeria* and you all are a part of Operation New Beginning." He spoke slowly and paused after each statement. "I have chosen each one of you because you all are some of the best at what you do. There are ten people aboard consisting of myself, engineers, scientists, and soldiers."

Watkins was quick to count and interrupted.

"Sir, I hate to be a stickler here, but I think a crew member missed the bus ride. I only see nine."

Goodwin grinned at Watkins.

"Ah, yes, Sergeant Watkins, my mistake. Let me rephrase myself. There are ten, well, crew members aboard. Our tenth is not technically human. It's our ship." Goodwin looked up. "Avi say hello to the crew."

"It's a pleasure," Avi said.

Goodwin took over again.

"She is our artificial vessel intelligence or Avi for short. She is in charge of getting us to our destination and making any decisions regarding our travel safety. Even though she is programmed to take orders, she can think and problem solve just as well as anyone on board."

Abruptly, Philips felt a rush of air against the back of his head causing him to turn his focus. The man sitting behind him had stood up quickly with irritation. All of the eyes in the cockpit were now fixed on him. He was an intimating individual with a dark, shaved head and two stern eyes. He was large, tan skinned, and each part of his body looked as if it were covered by some form of muscle. It was obvious to the crew that he spent a significant amount of time honing his body's strength. However, in spite of his build, it was not the reason why the crew focused their attention. The man's intention was to speak and everyone wanted to hear his stance.

With an audience, the large man spoke.

"Colonel Goodwin, are you telling me that a large amount of our safety is based off the decisions of artificial intelligence. You cannot seriously expect me to rely on an emotionless robot for judgments regarding my safety. This thing can't possibly make decisions regarding life because it can't possibly think like a human."

"Everyone, Marine Corporal Michael Daniels," Goodwin introduced with his hand held out. "Corporal, with all due respect, Avi deserves more credit than you give her."

Behind Goodwin was the mysterious man, who had stopped his play with the screens and begun to walk toward the crew. He resided next to Goodwin's side and looked directly into Daniels dark eyes.

"Actually," he started. "Avi is designed from human characteristics and even has her own personality. Her mental processing is way more advanced than yours or mine."

"And who might you be?" Daniels asked.

"Stephen Dover. I designed Avi and her body. So, technically, I designed the ship I guess you could say."

"Listen Mr. Dover, not to take away from your incredible creation, I just don't see how I could put my trust into something that does not truly understand the human condition. I think a robot would only give us more risk and danger. The damn thing would probably kill us if it had the chance."

Interrupting the two was Avi's unaffected voice echoing from the walls and ceiling.

"Corporal Michael Daniels." Avi had clutched the crew's attention. "A large amount of combat experience and mission success. Known for his unconventional yet affective combat skills. Received the bronze medal while serving in North Africa and of active Non-commissioned Officer, he holds one of the highest kill rates." Avi paused for a moment. "One could say Corporal Daniels expressed bravery and merit. What people fail to see is that his dangerous and gun hoe attitude has caused numerous risks among his own. For example, while under Daniels command, twenty-three soldiers died in combat just outside of Al-Jawf, Libya. Even though, he was never completely held responsible for the deaths, both he and the others who survived know it was a result of his greedy decision making."

Avi stopped talking to allow this information to sink into Daniels' head. Daniels was taken aback as he stood looking as if Avi had smashed an egg in his face. He had become the personification of humbled and had no ability to respond to the attack. However, Avi wanted the kill. She wanted to end his outburst and place him back in his seat. She truly interacted like a human expressing attitude and wittedness in order to defend her image.

"But please Corporal," she began to conclude. "Educate me on what the human condition is and how I can better understand how to protect a unit."

There it was, the killer blow that was Avi's verbal hook. Daniels never stood a chance against her quick remarks and in depth research. Knowing his limits, he admitted defeat by subtly nodding his head and returned to his seat. He had a growing thirst for the machine's blood, but he recognized that his time was not now. Daniels dreaded the cliché; however, he momentarily valued it. Avi had won the battle, but Daniels assured himself he could win this war.

"Well, I wasn't hoping to introduce everyone this way," Goodwin spoke once more. "Daniels is one of the best U.S. marines that should be recognized for his valor and bravery. But, as you all now know, Avi has done vivid research on each of your backgrounds. And you can thank Mr. Dover for that." The entire crew laughed except for Daniels, who sat in complete silence. "Back to my original speech. This ship consists of ten members. Our main objective for this mission is to find and claim a planet that we found in an isolated planetary system similar to our own."

"Meaning it has a sun-like star?" Thatcher chimed in.

"Exactly." Goodwin said as he turned himself with his hand meeting a holographic screen. With a few motions, the colonel revealed the image of a planet that Philips found strikingly familiar. "This is Exodus-114. From what we know, Exodus is a relatively new planet that's untouched and unexplored. We found the planet two years ago as a part of an R.P.S.E., or robotic probing spacecraft expedition. Upon its discovery, by what we like to think of as Avi's mother, we began to design a secret exploration mission. We have followed each of you for years so that we cou...."

"Excuse me Colonel," inquired an unheard female voice. "Hi everyone, Dr. Elizabeth Rodriguez," she introduced. "I am the geologist and meteorologist aboard."

Rodriguez stood from her seat next to Philips and had temporarily distracted his mind. His love for wife was strong enough to limit his lust, but her beauty was enough to clench his attraction. She was a gorgeous and brown skinned Latin American woman. Her long, brown hair was thick and pulled tightly into a tail by a small elastic band. Philips was stunned by the earth scientist's appearance. Her body was less like that of a scientist and more of an Olympic gymnast. Beauty was her true occupation for she could not have been more than thirty years of age with a face so seemingly perfect. Although she spoke quietly, her words flowed with a graceful Hispanic rhythm and tone.

"I can't help but notice how you mentioned it was a secret mission," she claimed.

"Yes, it is a secret expedition," Goodwin assured.

"Well, I, and I am sure the others as well, are somewhat curious as to why. After all our friends and family know that we are on this expedition. How secret could it be?"

"No one, other than this crew and our funding government, knows about Exodus. For all they know, this is just a routine exploration."

"But why must this be kept a secret from the world. Shouldn't people be embracing the potential?"

The colonel's face became noticeably serious.

"The government finds that this is best kept as a secret because we cannot risk this being taken the wrong way by other countries. They might see this as a power struggle which could initiate a conflict. This is the best way to keep peace among the world."

Philips sat forward from his chair as Rodriguez's toned physique found her seat once again. With his hand placed upon his chin, he thought and questioned the colonel's statements. He was glad that Rodriguez had addressed the possible issue of secrecy, but was left in disappointment with the response. Goodwin's answer was a legitimate answer with strong reasoning, yet Philips felt as though it were insufficient. Yes, he had only mentioned an exploration to his friends and wife, but there must have been more secrecy involved in this trip.

However, to Philips surprise, Goodwin had eased the tensions with his seemingly false affirmations. His reassurances were deceitful and cunning, but the crew was blatantly naive to the political campaign he was pitching before them. How was it, he thought, that none of the crew members could see Goodwin's possible alternative motives? Philips was able to see past his fabricated exterior, finding Goodwin's dark and devious eyes. His schemes were witty and conniving which would make it all the more necessary for Philips to find some form of proof.

Goodwin continued after noticing the crew was now at ease. "We have followed each of you all through your careers and believe that you all are the best fit for the mission." He changed the subject. "Our ship is the fastest ship that has ever been created. This means that we will be able to cover the light years it takes to travel to Exodus in a matter of months. According to Avi's calculations, we should arrive on Exodus within a little over two months. Upon arrival each of you will be expected to do exactly what you have been hired to do." Goodwin began to list each individual and their job descriptions. "Our scientists aboard are Dr. Elizabeth Rodriguez, our geologist, Dr. James Thatcher, physicist, and Dr. Adam Zuckerman, ecologist."

Philips had not noticed Zuckerman's presence before Goodwin's introduction. Zuckerman sat off to the side of Rodriguez; therefore, her presence blocked Philips's view of him. As he slightly bent forward he was able to catch a glimpse of the ecologist. His face was young like most of the crew and marginally pasty. His styled, light brown hair and skinny frame came together in such a way it made him look like a film or music star. Philips, drawn to Zuckerman's idiosyncrasies, watched him anxiously bounce his foot on his crossed knee. The continuous action made Philips feel as though at any moment the man would stand up and reveal a bomb he had concealed under his uniform. Philips hoped that this was not the case but rather he was just excited to be on a space craft. Either way his hyperactive appearance made his personality and perhaps his sanity questionable.

"In charge of our protection on Exodus are Sergeant D.J. Watkins and Corporal Michael Daniels. They are here as a precautionary measure. In charge of vehicle and weapons repair is Lieutenant Christian Philips." Goodwin paused and directly focused on Philips. "Lieutenant Philips, you are most-likely going to want to meet with Mr. Dover so that you can become acquainted with the vehicles and weapons aboard."

"Yes sir," Philips responded nodding in the direction of Dover. Dover, in acknowledgement, did the same.

"Finally," finished Goodwin, pointing to the back of the cockpit, "our head scientist, Dr. Nar Porter."

Porter stood behind the crew, near a window that separated him from space. Something struck Philips differently about Porter in comparison to the rest of the crew. He seemed calm and still with his arms at his side. Porter possessed a refined appearance due to the scarce gel that parted the front of his dark head. He did not speak or even acknowledge the crew as they looked in his direction. His young and light colored eyes expressed a feeling of hope, but the purplish bags beneath somewhat oppressed the expression. Philips detected something moving in Porter's milky hand. He could not decipher what it was so he looked harder in order to discern the object's identity. It was a gold coin of some sort that Porter was spinning and rotating in and out of his knuckles. The habit was fairly soothing to watch as it rolled stylishly throughout his hand. The motion continued for a while then came to a stop as Porter pocketed the coin into his uniform. Following Porter's action, Philips realized that everyone had already reverted their eyes back to Goodwin, who continued to speak.

Philips listened to Goodwin once more and realized that the rest of his debriefing was either filler or a lie. Instead, Philips had something else that was toying with his every thought. Who was that suspicious man stand behind the crew? He did not speak and, besides revolving the coin in his knuckles, he did not even move. Philips found that upon leaving the debriefing he had more questions than before. Not only did he doubt Goodwin's motives, but now he had suspicions towards the crew.

FRIENDS AND DOUBTS

Days had passed and Philips had not had a chance to be the on ship detective he predicted. His insecurity still whelmed his thought but had taken a back seat to life on earth. He was now a father and the image of his son had been more important than his inquisitiveness. It was somewhat of a break from his worries as he experienced his son's birth. He was not present but was able to view the birth from an enlarged holographic screen on his bedroom wall. The screen was a part of a transition wall that could act as a visual display or a window.

Despite not being fully present and having to watch through a video, the emotional atmosphere made it feel as though he were next to Alicia's side. Beyond the sweat and tears, she was truly beautiful. Philips wanted to never forget the sparkle in her eyes as she held his son, Simon. He was small and healthy. Philips imaged Simon's little beating heart as he watched Alicia and his new son stare into each other's eyes, with glowing, pink faces. Nothing was said and nothing needed to be said. The new life left Philips and Alicia breathless and seemed to steal away their words. The silence was pleasant and Philips felt lucky. He found it hard to consider it a blessing when he was not entirely sure what that entailed. Instead, he believed lucky was the better choice of expression.

His eyes never left the screen while he bent forward as if he were attempting to get closer to his family. As he leaned forward, his beaded necklace fell outside his uniform so that it was dangling in front. He blindly placed his hand on the necklace's cross and fondled it gently. With the cross in his hand, he formed a smile and felt a subtle sense of hope forming. The feeling that was so quick to grow was also quick to die. The screen became fuzzy and undistinguishable. He released the cross in his hand, and it fell swiftly to his chest. Not fully understanding how to use the monitor, he tried tapping and touching it in different areas.

"Alicia," he inquired.

But there was no response as she failed to hear or even see his presence. The signal appeared to further weaken and began to gradually fade to a black screen. Disheartened, he stood and placed the palm of his hand against the wall. He stood like a statue with his head toward the ground and his hoping heading in the direction of his vision. Philips remained in the pose until Avi's voice filled the air. As her voice made its way into his eardrums, he pulled away from the wall and stood normally.

"As you all probably know by now we have lost all connection with Earth," Avi began to explain. "I am not sure of the cause or source, but I will inform the crew once we regain signal."

Desperately, he found the cross that hung from his neck. He smoothed it with his fingers until he found a knot that connected the cross to the beads. It was a basic knot. With a quick sense of judgment, he placed his other hand upon the knot and began to untie it gently. He positioned it before his eyes, pinched between the grasp of his index finger and thumb, while he gawked at its insignificance. After a moment passed, he lowered his head and let out an elongated breath. Then he slipped the wooden cross into his pocket, allowing the rosary beads to stand alone on his chest.

For the first time, since their departure from Earth, he felt isolated. He had been cut-off from the only life he had known and had been thrown into a world of unknown. He hoped that he could be a part of exploration, but he had begun to lose this hope. Maybe he was overreacting, he thought, but the truth was he had not expected to be so far from humanity. He thought he would embark on the journey with the support from mankind. He had signed up to enlighten the human race, not stumble across more secrets. Despair was mounting in his mind. He decided to leave his room and walk the ship.

As he walked through the ship, he found that what he used to think as remarkable had now become bland. The hallways of the ship seemed endless and dull. Whenever he passed a window, he saw empty dark space. In fact, space had begun to reveal the darkness within himself, and it was extracting his demons. He had something haunting him, taunting his faith. He needed someone he could talk to; he needed someone he could trust.

Like a signal, there it was. He had been walking the seemingly endless halls for hours, but now it was clear. Before him was a door and a name tag on the wall next to it that read, D.J. Watkins. Without hesitation he pressed the door button. The door parted revealing Watkins. He was shirtless and looked as though he had just woken up. The only thing Watkins wore was his uniform pants and the dog tags and cross that rested on his toned torso.

"Philips, do you know what time it is?" Watkins jokingly asked.

"No," Philips smiled. They both knew that space caused a lost concept of time.

"What are you doing?" Watkins waved Philips to enter. "Come in and sit. You want a drink?" He grabbed two glasses and a bottle of liquor.

"Yeah, I would love one."

The two sat down together at a circular table with four chairs around it. Sitting at two opposite ends of the table, Watkins poured Philips a glass and slid it across to him. Philips caught the glass before it fell of the table. Its momentum shift splashed a few droplets to the table's pale surface.

"What should we toast to?" Watkins asked.

"New Beginnings."

Watkins caught on to Philips's subtle attempt at a pun and chuckled a little. Their glasses connected echoing a light ringing sound followed by the gentle sipping by both. The men mirrored each other with a widening of their mouths and a clenching of their teeth in order to tolerate the burning sensation.

"So New Beginnings?" Watkins probed. "What is your new beginning?"

"My son."

"Your son?"

"Yes, my son, as of a few hours ago."

"Just born? Congratulations! This deserves another drink."

Watkins reached for the bottle once more and poured into Philips's glass until the liquid reached the brim. He then pulled the bottle back towards himself, pressed it against his lips, and took a swig.

"Thanks," Philips said as he laughed at Watkins gregarious attitude.

"This is a big celebration. We need to have a party of some sort. We should get the colonel in here and some fine women. Oh, how about that, huh, huh, Rodriguez. She was hot. And hell, I bet that Avi thing is programmed to host such a spectacle."

Philips continued to laugh at Watkins's hysterics. He knew that coming to his room would be a good idea. He felt less cynical than before; maybe all he needed was a good time with a friendly person. Philips wished that he could have a view on life like Watkins—just a carefree outlook where everything can be seen as a positive. How could someone who had been through similar events as himself could be so unaffected? Then it hit him. His slight intoxication began to pull on his emotions, but it seemed to elicit something dreaded. It was his demons. It was his past.

"Do you ever think about Africa?" Philips interrupted.

"What like the continent?" Watkins joked but recognized Philips's seriousness. "I mean yeah. Probably just as much as most who fought."

"And it doesn't bother you?"

"Of course it bothers me, it's just that I choose to look at it in a different way than most people would."

"I fought next to some of the best men I have ever known. And I watched them be torn to shreds by bullets and explosions. There was so much death from so many different angles. I killed dozens of insurgents while my fellow soldiers and friends seemed to be picked off one at a time…"

Watkins listened intently, noticing the subtle aggression in Philips's voice.

"…Our authorities or government or whatever you want to call it had the chance to prevent it all. We were stuck in a hot zone, and they couldn't pick us up. They told us it was too dangerous to fly us out. The risk wouldn't be worth the reward." Philips paused and continued with an even softer tone. "The risk wouldn't be worth the reward. I watched brothers, husbands, and fathers die because they weren't 'rewarding' enough."

Philips and Watkins both continued to sip on their liquor filled glasses. One glass turned into two and two into four. There truly was no concept of time for them. All they had was the liquor and their stories.

"We were like sitting ducks," Philips continued. "The only reason I am here today is because a nearby unit picked up on our distress call and they intervened, killing the remaining insurgents…" Philips had a subtle tremble in his voice. "But it was too late… My entire unit was dead, except for me." He paused for a moment allowing his thoughts to catch up to his mouth. "I don't know why all this happens. I don't understand the hate that arises. Why is there so much conflict and hatred?"

"But that is humanity in general, Christian." Watkins began to express his wisdom and knowledge. "The truth is that that is what humans do. No matter how much we come together, there is always going to be conflict. And where there is conflict there is war. It's how you choose to look at it that changes things. You can glorify its horrible image or you can embrace its blessings."

It was amazing how Watkins could take such a grotesque and gloomy idea and basically turn the table. He could have found good within a plague. Philips's mind was randomly shooting thoughts through his head. Watkins could not have been human with such optimism. Something so dark as war and hatred could in no way be a blessing. Thinking was slowly becoming absent in Philips's mind, and he need to express the apprehensiveness within him. It poured from Philips heart.

"See that is what strikes me the most. How can death be a blessing? There is no such thing as a blessing. I doubt if there is even a god because why would a god create an evil such as war. Any faith, I had ever had, I had lost just from what I experienced that day."

"You and I differ in this sense, my friend. I don't see the destruction and death that occurred in Africa. I believe in blessings, and I see a blessing in disguise. I see the fact that I am still alive as a blessing. And for that I thank God every day. For all we know this could all be some mysterious lesson *He* is trying to teach us in his mysterious ways." Watkins glared directly into Philips's hopeless eyes. "God shows himself, you just need to know where to look."

There was a significant amount of silence following Watkins's comments—partially due to the liquor, but it was mostly due to the message behind his words. Philips sat with a blank stare directed towards the table. He had never truly opened up to anyone the way he did with Watkins. He could not even contemplate revealing this darkness to Alicia. The darkness he held deep down in his core was unforgettable and had scarred his soul. Revealing something of this magnitude, to his wife, might have killed her spirit and affection. The slightest hint of his doubt and loss of faith would be demoralizing to her. He could not take away her innocent persona; in fact, he thought it was his duty to protect her from such things.

Philips's spinning vision caused him to roll his head in a circular motion. While rolling his head, his eyes met Watkins'. They both displayed two blank looks with their eyes barely held open by their glazing eyelids. *It was late*, Philips thought, and there was nothing intelligent left to say. Philips struggled to stand but found it slightly easier to wobble. He bumped the table softly as he stood and gingerly saluted Watkins with his right hand. Watkins returned with a weak handed salute himself and walked Philips to the door. As Philips exited and took a few steps out into the hallway and turned. "Thanks D.J."

"Anytime," Watkins replied.

"Oh, I almost forgot—" Philips said as he recognized that he still had a partially filled glass in his hand.

"—Keep for the road," Watkins replied. "It is a long journey back to your room."

At first, the journey was a long and difficult one as Philips faltered and stumbled a little. After a few moments and sips, Philips found a consistency in his step as he focused harder. It was a lot of work, but it would soon pay off, however, not in the way he expected. He had begun to turn a corner and enter a new hall when he saw him. Before him, in the adjacent hall, was Goodwin. *What were the odds?* Philips considered as he pulled himself sloppily back behind the corner. He leaned past the wall to view Goodwin like a spy would during an undercover assignment. Goodwin was completely unaware of Philips and his hiding spot. His back was facing Philips, and he walked intensely toward a door at the end of the hall. The hall was extremely bright, or so it seemed to Philips, causing him to squint forcibly. On the door was a symbol that Philips had recalled. It was the restricted area symbol that had previously taunted him and his curiosity.

By the time Goodwin reached the door, Philips had hit a high in attentiveness. All of his focus was on Goodwin's actions. Quickly, Philips flew out of potential sight as the colonel turned and scanned the hall in every direction. Philips stood motionless behind the corner for a few moments and gradually poked his head out into the hall. Goodwin's back was to Philips again and he swiftly dialed in a numbered code on the keypad. The keypad welcomed the numbered sequence and the doors parted for Goodwin's entrance. Philips watched the doors return to their closed position, but he noticed the light in the center of the door was Green.

Without hesitation, he snuck down the neighboring hall trotting towards the door. He stood in the spot where Goodwin was few seconds ago. He took one last sip of the partially filled glass. *One final boost of liquid of courage*, he thought, setting the glass on ground next to a wall. He knew this was a slightly imprudent and intuitive idea, but the alcohol had to some extent masked his discretion. The doors parted for him and he entered instinctively.

Beyond the doors was a single hallway that was a purely lighted white rectangle. Philips connected it to the bright light that one might experience just before death. However, this bright light had two options. There were two doors that Goodwin could have entered. Philips was tentative to approaching and opening the doors because he did not want to reveal his covertness. Consequently, he had too much curiosity to abdicate from this occasion. He walked up to the doors and inspected them. It would be easier than he thought as he noticed the doors were not the typical doors that were consistent throughout the ship. They were fully covered by glass and appeared to be manually operated.

He disregard the set that had a darkness coming from its inside and focused his full attention on the one with a light inside it. He posted up against the wall as he did the corner previously and exposed the top of his head carefully. On the opposite side of the glass was a room. The room was small yet it held an apparent amount of significance. It was a bright and white room, similar to that of the hall, but was filled with microscopes, beakers, and other instruments of science. A laboratory seemed to be the best way to describe it. Even though it was an interesting room, it was not what was interesting Philips.

Philips had been drawn by the voices he heard from the laboratory room. Not only did he hear the voice of Goodwin but he heard a new and furtive voice. He had not heard this man's voice before and Goodwin's standing presence blocked Philips's sight of him. He attempted to shift his head around at different angels, but Goodwin's frame was like a wall preventing any sighting. Then he saw something familiar, something distinguishing. A hand from the man prodded just barely past Goodwin's wall-like side. Philips observed the upward facing palm and caught a glimpse of a twinkling reflection. It was a golden, rounded figure that caused Philips to sober up considerably. He recognized the coin before and would always be able to identify its subtle magnificence.

Goodwin now removed his wall-like appearance by walking closer to Dr. Porter. Porter sensed Goodwin's nearing presence and began to elegantly spin the coin throughout his knuckles.

Without looking at Goodwin, he spoke. "Please Colonel, I would prefer it if you do not come too close."

Philips stretched his neck as far as he could, exposing his head even further. Learning about their shadowy interaction was more important to him than the possibility of being caught, though being caught never really circulated through his mind because he felt confident. The backs that faced him ensured an inability to see him. Porter's head became his focus as it was directed downward. Philips could image Porter's eyes piercing through something that rested upon the table before him. Clearly Porter was working on something attentively, with his coinless hand severely yet patiently working.

"How close are we?" Goodwin asked.

"We?" Porter implied.

"How close are you?" Goodwin corrected himself.

"Well Colonel, this is a delicate process." Philips could detect the intensity in Porter's voice. "I don't want to put a timeline on it. It can't be rushed, because if it is rushed then there are mistakes. And we both don't want that to happen."

"Cut the games, Porter." Goodwin was obviously annoyed with Porter's acerbic answer. "We had a deal. You would have this completed and ready for use when we are on Exodus."

"Well, are we on the planet yet, Colonel?" Porter sardonically remarked.

"You know exactly what I mean, Porter. You have a little over a month to finish this project. If you don't finish upon our arrival, then our deal is off and you won't receive your share."

"See that's what you don't understand about me, Goodwin, I don't care about the money. I never cared about the money." Porter paused so that his statement would sink in Goodwin's head. "I want to create perfection."

Philips pulled away from visibility and leaned his back against the contiguous wall. He felt his mind fall from reality for a moment and explore the possibilities of Porter's aspiration. Perfection was such a broad term causing Philips to ask himself, *what could he mean*? Maybe it was Porter's intention to create something perfect for humanity—something that would make Exodus the perfect place for all humans to live. However, Philips could not quite grasp the idea of perfection. It was a simple word that had such a complex meaning. He was uncertain with Porter's claim but knew that whatever he meant the statement carried a great deal significance.

Goodwin had become extremely irritated with their collaboration but understood Porter as an asset. "Look, I need the virus to be ready upon arrival so we can begin the project. I can't delay the crew because that would only create even more suspicion. Goodwin settled himself and spoke in a poised manner. "So be honest with me. Will it be ready?"

With his eyes never shifting from whatever was in front of him, Porter informed Goodwin of the process.

"I am close. My encoding is almost complete. You will have yours, and I will have mine."

There was a pause between the conspirators, and Philips felt his unauthorized welcome overstayed. He sensed that there was nothing further that the colonel would be able to pry from Porter's mind. He did not feel it necessary for him to be caught while listening to small talk. With a stumbling hesitation, Philips headed down the hall and toward the unlocked entrance in which he came. His escape was continuous and through a series of befuddled turns until Philips eventually found his issued bed.

Though Philips thought it a clean get away, his tracks would beg to differ. For it was Watkins's modest departure gift that had tainted his escape. There the liquor stained glass sat against the wall Philips had set it. It was a simple mistake; however, it was just noticeable for the colonel to see. Goodwin caught a glimpse of the glass as he exited the restricted area himself. He picked it up holding it on the tips of his fingers. Reminisce of the golden liquid built up at the bottom of the glass as he tilted it to its side. His nose picked up its scent allowing him to recognize the identity. With one last drink, the colonel drank the liquid's presence from glass.

PATHS OF FAITH

Without a sense of conscious knowledge, a little over a month had past and *New Sumeria* would soon find its way onto Exodus. Despite this circumstance, Philips found it hard to express emotion, for it took too much energy. Although he tried to stay optimistic about the arrival and discovery on Exodus, space was destroying him mentally. Space was cold and lacked the warmth needed to comfort the human soul. Simply put, space, to Philips, was not meant for the sustenance of human life. It had in some way drawn out the dark truth that he had a lack of faith. Whether it was the fact that he had limitless time to think over his horrific past events or whether it was the doldrums and darkness of space itself, he had now realized it.

As a result, sleep had become just as non-existent as the interaction between him and his friends and family on Earth. During the nights, Philips would spend his time fighting the firm mattress by rolling from side to side. He wanted to experience a dream but could not do so. He lived in a nightmare. At first, it was physical; he could not sleep because he could not merely adjust to space. But after a while, the thought of sleep deprivation became engraved in his mind. It was almost as if he was willing himself out of sleep as punishment.

He knew he had an internal conflict; however, he thought it best to forget about it and keep it within himself. It was breakfast aboard the *New Sumeria*. The ship's small mess hall had become filled by its crew. As Philips sat down among the rest of the crew, he remained silent and reserved, hoping not to divulge his conflict in anyway. Philips typically sat with the crew, but he never really socialized like most of them. It was not that he was shy or socially peculiar, he just preferred to listen to the others expose their personalities. Every once and a while, he would have a story or fact to share, but for the most part it seemed as though the same individuals spoke.

Philips thought nothing of the meal as it began like any other usual meal they had shared together. He sat in the same corner spot at the table that he always sat at. Watkins was always seated to his right while Rodriguez and Dover sat across from them. On the other side of Watkins and Dover, the table was filled by Zuckerman, Daniels, and Thatcher. Daniels sat next to Dover while Zuckerman and Thatcher sat next to Watkins. The table was not large but not so small that the crew had to pack themselves into their seats tightly. It was a well-sized table that allowed each member to sit comfortably without violating anybody else's space.

The room was small, but it was big enough to hold two tables at a respectable distance to where one could not eavesdrop on a quiet conversation. Philips observed the table every time he sat down, and it always remained empty. He dismissed the question of why the entire crew had to sit together at one table. He simply considered it an attempt to build morale or not to get left out of some facetious gossip. Being a military man himself, he had hoped it was the former seeing that the latter was relatively immature.

He never once saw Colonel Goodwin or Dr. Porter even touch the mess hall floor. It was possible that the room was too much for them to bear, Philips thought as he examined its design. After all, the room was extremely bright with the entire ceiling cover with rectangular lights. At times, the intense light reflecting off of the dull white walls was very harsh on the eyes. There were no windows, just a series of bland walls, a ceiling, and a door. One of the walls was accompanied by a machine that acted like a giant, white refrigerator, which stored their meals. Next to that was a heating unit for cooking their meals, which shared the same white-color theme. In some sense, Philips could understand it if Goodwin and Porter did not eat in the room because of its appearance. However, realistically he knew that it was probably for the purpose of avoiding the crew.

The crew sat at the filled up table without speaking. This muteness was odd yet overlooked. They all seemed partially asleep being that they ate an early breakfast. Each person had a glass of water and metal tray that was filled with the same oatmeal-like goop they ate for every meal. On board there was no chef or caterer, it was simply the same flavorless mix of a solid and liquid meal. Philips and the other military personal did not necessarily mind it, but it was obvious the others were growing nauseous just from its sight.

Sharply, the sound of metal against metal contact rang throughout the room, echoing through the room's emptiness. The sound had come from Zuckerman's spoon being dropped on his tray. Though it was a small action it had a large sound that now turned the members into spectators

"I am sick of this stuff!" Zuckerman exclaimed.

Philips never really experienced a direct conversation between him and Zuckerman. He never really talked to anyone but had succeeded in making Philips uncomfortable following the debriefing. Even early in the morning, Zuckerman seemed restless and slightly irrational.

"Let's call in the five-star chefs for Zuckerman," Daniels joked, looking around the table.

Daniels had loosened up significantly following the quarrel between him and Avi. His pride was too great to let a machine get to him mentally.

"That's easy for you to say, considering that you are used to eating this kind of shit," Zuckerman returned as his head remained down in the direction of his mush.

"Don't worry, in a month or two you will be back enjoying your catered lifestyle with Rodriguez and Thatcher. I'm sure Mr. Dover will have built an accommodating robot for you two."

Of the three that were mentioned, Thatcher was the only one who took the comment personally. Rodriguez ignored it, and Dover, fascinatingly, thought of it as a compliment. Thatcher seemed as though he were the type of person that always defended his image. It was as though he need the attention and recognition of his scientific genius.

"What is that supposed mean?" Thatcher glared at Daniels across the table.

Daniels had obviously thought that being in the military made him an expert on character and strength. He believed he had earned the right to look down on those who he thought had lived a privileged life.

"Let's be honest, you scientists have an easy life."

"An easy life? When was the last time you wrote a book describing a complexity of the physical sciences?"

"When was the last time you had a bullet fly in your direction?"

"What, are you saying that because I don't have people shooting at me, I am privileged?"

"I am just saying you have never really had to fight for anything. Don't take it so personally."

"Don't take it so personally? You are deliberately trying to insult us for no reason."

The argument had become very childish. Philips looked around the table to see if anybody was actually listening to their banter. Watkins ate with his spoon in a tantalizing motion and a grin across his face while Dover simply sat back and viewed the show. The others did not seem so entertained by the disagreement and had different emotions. Both Rodriguez and Zuckerman ate with their heads down. Rodriguez was blatantly annoyed and she continued to exaggeratedly exhale so that the others could hear her breathing. On the other hand, Zuckerman acted like a frightened rodent cowering into his tray away from the tense voices.

Philips examined Daniels once more and easily concluded a verdict of him. He was nothing more than a bully. The fact that the United States Marine Corps would give him a position just seemed unbecoming. His presence seemed as though he would be more damaging than helpful. For all he knew, the marines trained him to physically and mentally break down the recruits and grunts.

"We should get the boxing gloves for you two," Watkins said as he bit down on his spoon and stared.

"Watkins, don't encourage them!" Rodriguez blurted out. She had grown tired of their bickering. "Can't we just eat?"

Rodriguez had put a halt on the argument and there was a temporary silence at the table. The silence was quickly broken by Daniels, who had to have the last word.

"Because we would definitely know who would win the fight."

Thatcher gave him a glare, and Rodriguez fell back to her seat in disappointment.

"Daniels!" she exclaimed.

Rodriguez, in some ways, was like the mother for the crew aboard. She was typically good at suppressing the disagreements the men of the crew had. Despite the age similarity among the crew, they all acted as though they were her children. Oddly Rodriguez accepted this role.

The silence that began earlier was present again; however, there was no interruption this time. They sat in complete silence and gradually finished their meals. Eventually, each individual began to clear out one at a time until Watkins and Philips were the only ones left behind. However, as they finished, Philips noticed the door part for someone entering. A couple double-takes and a series of blinks led Philips to the realization of who it was.

Nar Porter had made a rare and unanticipated appearance in the dining hall. He stood in place for a moment and looked around the room. Philips could tell that the lighting was getting to him as Porter squinted slightly. As his eyes shifted around the room they briefly met the inquiring eyes of Watkins and Philips. The connection was momentary but it had left Philips with a sense of acknowledgement and welcoming. Porter walked across the room and toward the refrigerator. In a sequence of actions he was able to construct his meal and sit at the unoccupied table.

Philips was observant of Porter's every motion and did not once take his eyes off the mysterious scientist. He had lasting suspicion following his drunken spying on Goodwin and Porter. He forgot about the majority of the interaction because they never truly revealed any tangible information. For the most part, the two were relatively broad. Nonetheless, he did question what Porter meant by his usage of the term perfection. At the moment he did not express any worry towards the conversation because he could not see a word such as perfection being detrimental towards him or the crew. In some ways, he was just curious as to what Porter had in mind and why.

Philips leaned in close to Watkins so that he could speak with a whisper. "I have to talk to him."

"Why?" Watkins questioned.

"I don't know. There is just something about him."

"All right, I guess. I will see you later," said Watkins as he stood from the table and made his exit out of the room.

Watkins acknowledged Philips's personality for what it was, inquisitive and interested in finding whatever truth he thought was hidden. He knew Philips was the type of person who would never be fully satisfied until he found the answers for himself. It was as if he needed to hear every facet of a story before he could make a final verdict. He never took the word of mouth as fact, unless it came from the actual source. Watkins had an understanding towards Philips's fixation for knowledge and assurance. In no way did he want to hinder it; deep down he admired the quality.

They both stood up with Watkins matriculating towards the door, and Philips gradually making his way to the table where Porter was sitting. For a moment, Philips looked up at Watkins as he passed through the parted doors and they shared a final departing gesture. Philips shifted back to Porter and had now been standing just before the chair that sat across from him. He pulled the chair out slowly with his eyes fixed on Porter and steadily composed himself into the seat. Not even the slightest glance made it across to Philips. Porter was consumed with something before him. Philips found this to be a recurring theme with Porter's conversations as he had observed the same actions previously.

A piece of paper and a pen were keeping Porter occupied while Philips sat waiting for some form of interaction. Philips inspected the paper Porter was absorbed into. He was drawing a picture like a young child would with a batch of crayons. There must have been more to it since a man of Porter's profession would not typically draw childish pictures. Then again, Philips doubted, he knew nothing of his personality and his sanity. In an effort to induce any form of attention, Philips cleared his throat. Even though it was not what Philips had copiously hoped for, the truism worked to some extent.

Porter continued to draw but acknowledged. "Lieutenant Philips."

Philips was somewhat staggered that Porter had known his name, despite their long travels. He assumed that Porter would not have remembered his name, considering the two had never had any form of contact.

"Dr. Porter," Philips addressed.

Porter continued to work on his penmanship, burning through the paper. There was a long pause between the two as he thought that Porter would direct a question to him. Yet, nothing was asked and Philips grew anxious to the point that he needed to disrupt the silence. Porter expressed no interest in anything other than the masterpiece. Philips had, to that point, received just as much consideration as Porter's untouched, grey meal.

Abruptly, Porter dropped the pen from his hand. It landed softly on the inscribed piece of paper. He let out a sigh of relief and pulled the front of his medium-length and fair brown hair back to the center of his head, resting his hands atop. His eyes were still fixed on his masterpiece, but he did not hover over it aggressively. Instead, he now pressed his back against the chair and progressively lifted his eyes until they met Philips.

Porter studied him beyond what Philips could not see himself. He knew that Porter's eyes were doing more than looking at him. They examined him so deeply that they seemed to burn through his core and extract any previously unattainable personal information. He wanted to prevent Porter's clairvoyant abilities and in order to do so he needed an action that would distract him temporarily. He believed that action was through conversation. Though it was not the ideal way of starting a conversation, it was the only thought that came to his mind.

"I am curious," Philips began to ask, "What kind of name is Nar Porter?"

Porter had become slightly disgruntled by the fact that Philips had ended his analysis, but he indirectly acknowledged Philips's clever refuge. "After all, Porter is common but Nar seems as though it wouldn't be a typical," Philips paused in order to check his appropriateness. "It wouldn't be a typical, well, Caucasian name."

Porter smiled a little and entertained the question with a story. "Well, you are right" he cleared his throat and continued. "My real name is Narayan. It is a Sanskrit-based name." He somewhat regrettably sighed and revealed further information regarding his name. "However, as you and I both know, a name so different as Narayan would never last in grade school. So when I was young I ended up changing my name to Nar in hopes of making my name seem, well, more American."

Narayan? Philips thought as the name rolled off the tip of his tongue smoothly. He was unfamiliar with the name, but he never really thought much of its meaning.

Porter persisted with his story after clearing his throat once more.

"See, I never knew my father, but my mother, I somewhat did. She was an American. A successful sociologist in fact. She loved to travel the word and explore varieties of cultures and religions. She would collect what she had gathered from these places and used it in her everyday life. Whether it was the things she bought and found or it was the knowledge she gained, she would always open-mindedly practice it in some way." Porter, realizing he had digressed considerably. He rethought and put his words back on track. "When my mother spent time traveling in India, she had come across a young man named Narayana. Narayana had taken care of my mother while she was pregnant and taught her about Indian philosophies and teachings. She became, I guess you could say, inspired. Because of his guidance, the name *Narayana* stuck with my mother so much that when it came time to name me, she gave me the name Narayan."

Philips sat with a glazed look in his eyes but was conscious and fully aware of Porter's story. He had been engulfed into a sudden world of characterization and travels. All of which came from the story-telling magic that Porter had so modestly possessed. Philips was surprised to such an in-depth story following such a simple question. However, his astonishment was due to the fact that he had never expected Porter to open up to him so quickly. This conversation was the first interaction the two had shared and yet he found himself following a story of Porter's origin.

Philips exhaled sharply and shortly, almost like a concealed laugh. "That was truly a remarkable story. Your mother sounds like an extraordinary individual."

"Sounded," Porter corrected.

"Sounded?" Philips asked confusedly.

"She died months after my birth." Porter sighed. "She had dengue fever from her time spent in India."

"I am sorry to hear that," Philips sincerely expressed. Oddly, Porter did not seem very fazed.

"It's fine," he assured. "I didn't even know her really. In fact, what I told you were merely stories from my family and her friends."

Philips felt a sense of maladroitness following his partial slip of the tongue. There they sat, staring deeply with their blank faces. Philips seemed intent on forcing Porter to speak so that the awkwardness would end. Growing gradually impatient again, Philips shifted around in his seat, moving himself in a way that gave him a better view of Porter's informal oeuvre. It was a spiral-looking design with two matching lines in length that wrapped around and mirrored each other. Inside the lines were more lines that were perpendicular and extended entirely across the original set. Philips could not see the detail written inside, but he could gather the idea of what it represented. Knowing well what it was depicting, Philips saw the opportunity to lead away from the awkward silence.

"What's that you are working on?" Philips asked.

Porter understood his attempt at conversation but answered shortly. "It a DNA molecule."

"Interesting. So what is it for?" Philips quickly pried.

"Let's just say I have an idea. Something that will have the ability to change the way people think."

"Think about what?"

Philips's questions had become quick and relatively thoughtless. They resembled similar questions that a young child would ask for the purpose of receiving attention. Even though he did not want to seem annoying in the eyes of Porter, he did crave any form of attention that Porter would give him. He wanted to learn all he could about the mysterious Dr. Nar Porter, for this moment could be their only encounter.

"Life," Porter inquired. "And the flaws that come with it."

Philips recognized this thought.

"What do you mean?" He paused for an instant. "Are you talking about…perfection?"

Following the spoken words, Porter's eyes grew large and bright. He had the appearance of a child experiencing a toy store for the first time in his life. A glow encompassed his body and radiantly expressed his joy with the word. Perfection was simply a word, but its meaning had created an abundant amount of energy in Porter's body. Philips could feel it transferring its momentum through the air and across the table into himself. He knew he had struck gold.

Hiding some of his remaining excitement, Porter attempted to change the topic in order to not reveal his plans.

"So what brings a Lieutenant, such as yourself, on this mission?"

Philips noticed Porter's sudden avoidance of any dialogue about perfection and realized he needed to rethink his direct approach. Porter was playing a game with Philips; however, Philips was still learning the rules. He needed a game changing question or comment that would trap Porter into the perfection mind set. It was becoming back and forth, like a battle between a pitcher and batter where Philips would have to find the pitch that would get Porter to swing. For now, though, he would amuse Porter's change of topic with a subtle bluff.

"Where do I begin…" Philips started, expressing his newly reinvigorated poker face. "Exploration, discovery, I joined this mission because there is the potential for humanity to develop beyond what is capable."

Porter examined him deeply. "Is that all?"

"I mean those are some big things Dr. Porter, I don't know what could be more important in my mind."

"Do you have a wife?"

Philips was taken aback by the seemingly random question, but he was still familiarizing himself with the game.

"Yes," Philips answered.

"Children?"

"A newborn son."

Porter smirked, giving Philips the feeling that he had said too much.

"See what I mean? Porter started. "There is more to it. Exploring and being humanitarian are not big enough motivations to draw a husband and a father multiple light years away from his family. There is something greater—something that fuels you."

It was truly an uncanny vibe that rushed through Philips's body. He had heard that Porter was a smart man, but his questions had somewhat of a supernatural feeling to them. Porter had become a parasite within Philips's body. He could sense him squirming throughout his brain, stealing every thought and memory. There had been a sudden change in events and now Porter was miles ahead of Philips.

"I have come to notice in the world that people don't become motivated unless there is a benefit for themselves in some way," Porter informed. "People may say they might be doing something for the 'greater good,' but the truth is everyone acts in terms of themselves."

"I find that hard to believe, Dr. Porter. What about people who volunteer to help the sick and dying or those who fight in wars for their countries? Are you telling me these people are acting in favor of themselves?"

"Exactly. You only see the exterior of these people. You do not see what is deep down below the core. Those who volunteer might do so in order to be recognized by others as being a good person while those who fight might want the glory. There are hidden motives for every seemingly selfless act. Whether it is for money or social image, the truth is people are naturally selfish."

"That may be true for some, but I know for a fact that I am here because I want to improve humanity. I want to enhance our knowledge and growth. I wouldn't consider that selfish."

Porter leaned forward allowing his crossed forearms to rest upon the table. His face had become the most serious Philips had ever seen it. "Lieutenant," he said with a deep and extremely low tone. "You left your family at a time when they needed you the most. And you did so for a space expedition. I wouldn't consider that selfless." Porter paused and cocked his head to the side barely.

"But that's not it," he said slowly shaking his head but continuing to hold his studying stare. "There is something else. Why are you here? It's not for the money and I can assure you that this human advancement bull is a cover-up. You probably don't know it yourself, so you tell everyone the same line. It's ironic because most people know they are covering up their true motivations in some way or form. Look at the people on this ship now. Each individual is being paid five million dollars apiece to travel on the ship and explore a planet they have never heard of. But, if you ask them why they are doing this, then they will all give you the same answer. Human discovery, exploration, adventure, etcetera, etcetera. However, I can assure you that they all have the same warm feeling upon the mention of money. Simply take away the money and there would be no crew for the *New Sumeria*. There would be no mission. No ship. No effort. Nothing."

He let the word *nothing* ring for moment so that Philips was forced to think of it and its significance. Porter relaxed himself to the back of his chair with his arms still folded. Calm and posed he seemed; nevertheless, his words held so much energy and passion. His arguments were fairly resilient, but they were not for the purpose of proving himself right. Instead, he hoped to influence Philips in a way that would possibly bring him closer to an intellectual enlightenment. Porter was not flaunting his intelligence; he was helping Philips see his own hidden incentive. In a way, it was Porter's gift to Philips.

"But, with you it is something else," Porter continued.

Philips attempted to redirect the attention. "How about you? What brings you on this ship? Where does your incentive come from?"

"I told you already," he said as he lifted his chin. "You already know why I am here."

Philips was not entirely sure that he knew what Porter was referring to and did not truly understand why he was on the mission. He expressed the need to impress Porter and believed the only way to do so was to not expose his own ignorance. Without much of a thought towards their full conversation, he merely assumed that Porter's incentive was the money. In doing so, Porter had unintentionally steered Philips away from any suspicions about his real enticement. Though Porter had briefly mentioned his true motivation, Philips disregarded its minor reference and stuck to his assumption.

"Money. Just like everyone else aboard," Philips stated with confidence.

"Just like everyone else." Porter said and directed the attention back to Philips. "But you. You don't care for the money. The government could have paid you with a rock and a stick and you would have still found your way aboard this ship. And you may not see it yet, but human discovery did not bring you here."

The darkness within Philips was now returning as he could feel its presence once again. *Was Porter right?* He thought to himself. Philips had been telling everyone that he had wanted to come on this exploration on the behalf of humanity. However, maybe it was something subconscious that was creating this desire. He looked down to his chest, near his heart, but there was nothing there.

Porter caught a glimpse of Philips looking down toward his torso and thought intensely. He had recognized that Philips was looking for something there, but his dejected facial expression showed he could not find it. Intent on finding what it was, Porter examined his uniform and found an outline. He visually traced the outline deliberately as if his eyes left a stream of color following their sight. The outline was that of a beaded necklace, one that was typically accompanied by a symbol. It lacked a key ingredient in its design. There was no small figure shaped as though it were to hold a human body of scale. The simple and basic shape, that holds an intricate meaning for most, was absent. Physically and spiritually, nothing hung from its interwoven grace. He continued to follow the lines of the beads as they spread a part only to come back together behind Philips's neck. His eyes shifted upward so that they were staring directly at the top of his head.

"Are you a religious man, Lieutenant?" Porter asked.

Philips eyes slowly moved upward away from his blank chest and met Porter's.

"No."

"And yet you wear prayer beads around your neck. To be honest, I find that quite interesting. Why would a man wears a rosary that is lacking a cross?"

"It was a gift from my wife. I promised I'd wear it for her."

"The necklace or the symbol?"

There was a pause in their interaction as Philips failed to provide Porter with an answer.

"Excuse me for prying, but I am just curious." Porter had his suspicions.

Although Philips was somewhat annoyed by Porter's questioning, he did not let it bother him. He would have rather uncomfortably allowed Porter to catechize him about his faith, or lack thereof, than to scare him away with an outburst. He too was attempting to interrogate Porter and learn information about him and possibly the mission. His own curiosity was more important than the luxury and contentment of the conversation's atmosphere.

"It's perfectly fine," Philips admitted. "I just have my doubts."

"Your doubts?"

57

"I mean, I have the feeling that I want to believe. But…" Philips could not connect his thoughts clearly and was stopped in his speech.

"What happened?" Porter asked with a dark glare. "You obviously used to believe."

"North Africa happened, doctor." His eyes seemed to grow worrisome. "I saw too much death and destruction. I can't find faith in a world of so much darkness."

"I see."

"How about you, Dr. Porter? What do you believe?"

Porter chuckled. "Me? Come on, Philips, I am a scientist." The claim was meant to be a joke, but Porter was only able to draw out a quick smile from Philips's face. Recognizing Philips's seriousness, Porter became stern as well. "I have no belief. I never had a belief in any faith, and I never will."

For some odd reason, Philips sensed dishonesty in Porter's voice. He found it hard to believe that Porter had never once experienced even the slightest feeling of faith. From the way he talked about it, it seemed as though he had never questioned the existence of human life. He just seemed to accept it for what it was and did not inquire from where or what did humanity and its elements come from. It was an essential thought that had to have crossed everyone's mind at some point in their life. This thought should have been especially prominent in Porter's head, considering he was a scientist.

Philips questioned his honesty and somewhat attempted to elicit it through talk of himself.

"But I become disheartened, in a way, because I feel as though everyone has to have some kind of faith in something."

Porter had palpably become annoyed and spoke on the topic in the direction of himself.

"Do you want to know where my faith lies? It lies within myself. I have faith in myself and no one else. No imaginary figure or figures that people choose to believe in. People put so much time and effort into meaningless symbols, for what? Failure and let down. For all I care, I could put all my faith into this coin."

Philips had not noticed it before, but in Porter's hand he held his signature golden coin. He must have held it in his non-writing hand, for Philips could not see it prior to his mentioning. The coin separated the two men, pinched between Porter's index finger and thumb. He certainly detained an amount of value in the coin considering that Philips had always seen him with it in his hand. Porter might have joked about his faith resting in the coin, but the fact that it was constantly with him gave the joke some truth.

A silence grew following Porter's statement. Mostly because Porter had anticlimactically left his speech and returned to his analysis of Philips. It was obvious Philips was in deep thought, but Porter expressed intent on finding his thought's source. He had remembered Philips explaining that he had no faith or belief, but he also remembered his mention of disheartenment from his lack of faith. Thinking for a moment, it came to him. Porter had figured it out. He knew the answer that he had been in search of. It was so clear to him he had grown slightly disappointed with himself and his inability to previously put his finger on it.

"No, no," Porter started. "I see it now. You say you don't believe, but the truth is you don't know. You want to believe in a god, but your past fills your head with disbelief."

Philips became worried, he felt a sense of apprehension that Porter might reveal some truth—a truth that might oppose any benefit and possibly carry more darkness. He knew that in his weak state, he would be vulnerable to Porter's words. However, he felt a desire to listen to Porter's explanation of Philips's spiritual condition.

"You left Earth because you were in search of your own faith," Porter explained. "You took this job to escape the evils that humans can so copiously display—a hope of escaping it all. But you want to believe, you want to put your faith in a higher being.

And you thought you could find your faith by finding human goodness. In your mind, it is the hope for humanity to come together through exploration and discovery." Porter chortled concisely. "Simply, you could not find your salvation on Earth so you thought you could find it somewhere else."

Philips attempting a final stand against Porter's claims spoke. "So you think that I believe I would find my faith by traveling to a distant planet light years away. That's extremely impractical."

"Exactly my point, Mr. Philips. You just don't know it yet."

"Know what?" Philips asked defensively.

"You will realize that your desire for faith had brought you on this mission. But be forewarned that you are headed down an endless road. I will be the first to tell you that this expedition will not give you faith. This expedition won't change anything."

Abruptly, their conversation was disrupted by the door of the room parting into the walls. On the outside of the doors was a familiar, yet surprising face that made its way through the rectangular door way. Philips had thought it to be a lucky sighting catching Porter in the room; however, he thought it outlandish to see Colonel Goodwin standing in the room as well. Philips had never seen either one of the two in the mess hall before and would have disregarded it if he was told.

Despite Goodwin being the oldest man aboard, he had look as though he was healthy and well-rested as he stood with his unyielding posture. Everyone else aboard had seemed to age and wither by five years upon their departure. However, space and its travel were in a way Goodwin's natural Botox. With his age-defying look, he held a stern face as though he were irritated by something. He directed his eyes at Porter for a moment without saying anything. It was as if the two were telepathically speaking to one another. After the moment of visual communication, the colonel turned toward Philips and spoke.

"Lieutenant Philips, I was hoping I would find you in here. We are assembling all the military personal to meet with Dover this morning for a weapons and technology debriefing."

Philips connected his eyes with Goodwin's. "Yes sir. Where is this debriefing?"

"You will meet in the Ordnance Room," he informed. "Oh, and try to not get lost. I would hate to have to clean up after you again."

WEAPONS AND INTELLIGENCE

With each step, Philips's legs acted as gears pumping and activating the flow of his thoughts. While the white, brightly lit hallways seemed to brighten his mind as well. It was a long walk to the ordinance room; however, the trip would most likely take twice the time it normally would. The heaviness of Philips's head had slowed his pace considerably. Nonetheless, he needed the distance, environment, and pace. He needed this time to puzzle a few ideas together. Coincidence was too modest of a word to describe Colonel Goodwin's oddly timed entrance into the mess hall. His visitation must have held some purpose or reason because Philips understood that everything is cause and effect. Still, he knew that the question was not whether or not Goodwin had purpose for his entry. The question was why.

His mind had now fallen into a volleying of emotions. In a single series of steps he found himself continuously alternating between anxiety and relief—an uncanny combination of emotions for most. However, it was an appropriate description of his status. His nervousness had somewhat always been present ever since the departure of the ship, but it was heightened following Goodwin's peculiar timing. He stopped walking for a moment and stood in front of a glass visual of space. Looking through the window and onto the black blanket, he recognized the number of random and unidentifiable stars that were dispersed.

Goodwin's reason for his interruption was similar to the stars in the sense that it was unlimited. Scanning them slowly, Philips focused his eyes upon a single star, as he tried to minimize and limit his reasoning. Philips thought that it was as if Goodwin was attempting to prevent any dialogue between Dr. Porter and himself. He assumed that ordinance room debriefing was an excuse to force him away from Porter. And what of the comment Goodwin made just prior to his departure? *Try to not get lost. I would hate to have to clean up after you again,* he replayed through his head. The comment seemed irrelevant, but it was likely that he would not make the connection, considering his intoxication had eliminated any remembrance of the glass he had left behind.

He returned to his slow walking pace once more with his sight on the hall. He now focused on the other emotion he was experiencing, relief. *A surprising emotion,* he thought to himself, but it made sense at the same time. Goodwin had ironically saved him. Prior to Goodwin's hasty entrance, Philips had been experiencing a mental assassination attempt by Porter. If it were not for Goodwin, Philips could have possibly ended up brain dead.

Suddenly, his train of thought was broken by a calling from behind him.

"Christian," the voice identified, interrupting his scattered thoughts.

Philips recognized the voice and the fact that there was only one person aboard who typically called him by his first name. It was that of D.J. Watkins, his other savior. This time Philips was being saved from his own mental destruction; for his brain was firing on all cylinders and driving him mad. He had, in a way, become his own worst enemy as his thought process had shifted from suspicion at the start of the mission and more towards insanity. Though he knew it purely to be a mental fixation, he attributed it to him gathered more and more questions and not answers.

He stopped and turned to pinpoint the voice, already knowing who it belonged to. To his surprise, there was another individual standing next to his light-hearted friend. He acknowledged Daniels based on his muscularly built physique. The two gradually made their way towards him, to the point that they stood inches from one another. Philips looked directly at his Watkins.

"Weapons debriefing?" Watkins asked.

"Yes," Philips returned.

"Very good, let's go."

Considering that the three had stopped to talk just a few hallways away from the ordinance room, the rest of the walk was brief. They entered the bus-sized door to the room one at a time. Philips's head circled, capturing the essence of the even larger room. Similar to the rest of the ship, it was a bright room sharing the bland white coloring theme. On the left side of the room, there was a long firing range that was separated by a glass wall that stretched to the top of the high ceiling. At the front of the firing range was a racking structure that was attached to the wall. The rack held a countless number of stylish guns and an abundance of ammunition. To the right of the firing range was a gigantic open area about double the size. The area was consumed by the white color and appeared to be empty other than two vehicles, which Philips had recognized from before, when he had originally entered the ship's bay.

There was one of each vehicle and each shared an unsurprisingly white shade upon their exterior. The terrain vehicle sat on four wheels that were to the height of Philips's navel. Each wheel had visible, spiraling shocks that were black and relatively long. It had a sleek design with stylish head lights in front, four vertically opened doors on the side, and a smooth hatch-back backside. A similar sleekness was apparent with the aerial vehicle to its right. It too shared the same white shade and looked as if it were originally a helicopter that had its blades replaced by wings. Underneath the wings were two identical circular pads—a common sighting for the people of their generation, for the pads were the gravitational lifts responsible for making it hover.

Alternatively, the rear was encompassed by two thrusters with a short tail in between to give it horizontal velocity.

His attention of the vehicle's design was ended due to the distraction of a sound coming from its blind side. Philips and the two others made their way to the opposite side of the aerial vehicle in order to find the source of the sound. Following the sound, they found Mr. Dover working diligently. The sound had come from the welding device that Dover was using to fix the side of the vehicle.

"Mr. Dover," Philips said. "We were told by Colonel Goodwin you were expecting us."

"I actually wasn't, but are you guys here for training?" Dover asked.

The fact that Dover was not expecting Philips and the others provoked an idea in his head. He was now assured had that Goodwin was simply trying to get rid of Philips earlier. Philips no longer needed to assume that Goodwin was using the debriefing as an excuse. It was a clear fact now that Goodwin wanted to prevent Philips from speaking to Porter; however, the reason why was still unknown.

"If you aren't busy..." Watkins chimed in.

"—No, no of course not," said Dover. "I have things I want to show you all anyways, but it will most likely be short. I have to prep for landing soon."

Dover stood up, grabbed a flat hand held device, and tucked it gently underneath his arm. He directed the group with his head as he walked past them and around the front of the vehicle. Now walking out in front, he kept his eyes forward and spoke without looking at them.

"Most of these weapons will be relatively refreshing," he said. "We were able to put a spin on some of the military's standard guns."

"Spin, how so?" Daniels inquired. "Aren't our guns already good enough?"

"Yes." Dover laughed. "But there is nothing wrong with a little more power and speed."

"Makes sense. But how?" Daniels asked.

"Ah, if I told you all my secrets, then I would lose my innovative value."

As they approached the firing range, Philips noticed that Dover's direction was toward the racking structure that he examined before. The rack was recognizable considering that it was the only black object against the colorless shaded wall. Across its base were similar guns that Philips had seen and possibly used before. The group now stood in front of its brilliance as he felt a chill echo its way through his body. There was something about the presence of a gun that gave him a feeling of exhilaration. He examined the rack in depth and imagined himself lightly pulling the soft trigger with his finger. Although he hated their somewhat inevitable conclusion in combat, he loved their design and refinement.

"Here's what's first," Dover said as he ripped a rifle off the rack, handing it to Philips.

Philips felt his excitement building as its texture and weight perfectly rested in his hands. The rifle's weight was light and its surface almost felt plastic to the touch.

Dover elegantly moved his fingers in a sequence against the side of the rack. An unlocking sound resonated around the group, capturing the eyesight of them all. Dover took a step back and another rack slid out to the left side of the original, exposing even more ammunition. Dover grabbed a magazine from the newly visible rack and handed the smoothly curved rectangle to Philips. Without hesitation, Philips snatched the magazine and snapped it into the rifle. He then pulled its side quickly causing a double-clicking sound to echo through white room.

"Yes, similar isn't it, Lieutenant?" Dover asked as he handed Watkins and Daniels handguns and ammunition. All three then received goggles and ear coverings. "Now, you may think these are

standard military weapons, but they are lighter and hit harder."
As everyone put on their protective equipment, he looked at
Philips directly. "Go ahead, Lieutenant."

Philips turned to the end of the firing range and walked
towards it barely, so that he was at the top. He pushed the end of
the rifle deep into his shoulder until he felt its pressure cut-off his
arm's circulation. His opposite arm tightened his fingers around a
holding attachment that jutted downward. Though he could not
feel the attachment because of his prosthetic arm, he could sense
its grip based on the steadiness of the weapon. Cocking his head
slightly, he placed it just before the scope that securely resided
upon its top.

As his eyes refocused, he examined the gun briefly. It was truly
a nimble and agile piece of equipment. Its smoothness on every
straight edge and angle gave it a weightless feeling. With his
sight now directed through the scope and towards the center of
the target, Philips softly and gradually pinched the trigger. The
rifle let off a series of short and concise purring rhythms.

"What do you think?" Dover called out loudly, just as Philips
had finished.

Dover's voice pulled Philips's head slowly away from the sight
of the rifle's scope. His vision adjusted from down the barrel to
the target that hung from a distance. The body-sized rectangular
target swayed back and forth for a moment. With its center
completely ripped open, the target had received the weapons full
bellicosity. Suddenly, it plummeted to the ground sounding like
a car door closing with force. He lowered the gun and turned his
head just barely over his shoulder but enough so that he could
see Dover. He stared without saying a word and cracked a grin.

"It seems you like it," Dover said returning the smile.
"Gentlemen, care to try."

Both Watkins and Daniels made their way to where Philips
had been shooting from. Philips did the opposite. His gun found
its way back into the rack and he settling himself where the others

stood. After the target Philips had torn to shreds was replaced, the firing began once more.

As the two fired next to one another, a mixing pot of sounds rang from the air. Sounds of quick, subtle explosions mixed with series of repetitive popping to create the orchestra of war. When the firing subsided, there was a grand finale of metal chiming as the bullet showered from their targets. Following the loud excitement, Watkins and Daniels returned to the racks. They followed Philips's action by replacing the empty slots on the wall with their weapons.

Once everyone had settled, Dover spoke to the group. "They are similar to what you guys typically use, but like I said, we just put a spin on it." The group lightly laughed. "For the most part, that is it for you two," he said in the direction of Watkins and Daniels. "The rest is for Philips."

Dover walked up to Philips and placed his hand on his shoulder. The gesture was meant to be somewhat of a guide as Dover directed Philips back to the vehicles, in which they stood by before. Watkins and Daniels training was extremely short, but Watkins still acknowledged Philips as they made their way out of the ordinance room. His acknowledgement was the same he had given earlier in the day upon their first departure. It had somewhat become a recurring action between the two.

As the pairs walked in separate directions, Dover informed Philips of his task.

"I have to introduce you to our two vehicles aboard. Also, how to access and work with Avi."

The comment did not carry much information; however, Philips had noticed that it had caught the attention of Daniels. He could see Daniels looking back at them as he exited the room. Philips knew that simply the name Avi would trigger his attention. Ever since Daniels and Avi's original encounter, Daniels had held a grudge towards her. In a way, Philips grew troubled by the thought because Avi was essentially the ship. It was as though Daniels had intentions on destroying the intelligence that ran the space craft. He did not doubt Dover's ability to control the ship, but he did not want their space expedition to be further complicated.

With the vehicles before them now, Philips let all else slip his mind and focused on the immediate task. Dover approached the terrain vehicle first and hopped into its driver's seat. Philips found it appropriate to follow the action by seating himself in the passenger's seat. As the two sat inside the machine, Philips examined its interior. The inside was simple for a supposed space vehicle, but Philips had little interest either way. He had had enough experience with four wheeled vehicles on Earth and did not need much lessoning.

"This is what we like to call the G.U.V. or ground utility vehicle. It is designed to handle any rocks and bumps Exodus might throw at us." Dover recognized Philips's slight boredom. "Relatively basic."

"It seems like a basic manual automobile," Philips returned. "I could operate and fix this."

"Good, but the only difference is you can communicate and gain assistance from Avi through this screen."

Dover pointed toward the center of the G.U.V. Above the shifting knob was a screen that projected an illuminating blue hue across their faces. With a series of hand gestures, similar to the ones he used during the launch, Dover pulled up a visual that presented itself on the dashboard. It was a blue holographic image of what appeared to be a woman's head. The appearance was gentle and sophisticated while its face was soft and young. In its medium length, the hair waved and swayed as it moved. Though it was an image, it held all the basic quality of a human.

Dover had expressed an even brighter glow than the blue that projected on the two.

"This is Avi," he explained.

"Avi is visible?" Philips asked with a puzzled face.

"She is more than visible, Lieutenant. Remember she can think just like us. Everything that is in front of her she can see and react to."

Avi turned her head and looked at Philips. "Hard to believe isn't it, Lieutenant," she said smiling.

"So you can access Avi from anywhere on ship or from any vehicle?" Philips asked.

"Basically," Dover responded.

"So why don't the people aboard know about her and let alone see her?"

"Well, I know about her, the colonel knows, and you now know, so I wouldn't say people don't know. Besides, I can't have Avi answering everyone at one time. If people knew about this, they would be exploiting it. No offense Avi."

"None taken," Avi smiled.

"I don't fully understand, you said she can only be at one place at a time?" Philips inquired. "I thought she was the ship."

"Well, yes and no. She is like any other person aboard. She is always thinking and controlling the ship, but she can only be in one area at a time physically, just like you or me. Think of the ship as her mind, she can control and sense her thoughts."

Dover pressed the screen with his index figure and Avi's face disappeared. The blue illumination slowly faded away until both their faces were returned to their original fleshy tone. Stepping out of the vehicle was Dover, with Philips following. He assumed that Dover would make his way over to the aerial vehicle but he instead started toward the door. Realizing that Dover was not in his presence, he turned to find him.

"Aren't we going to this one next?" Philips hollered at Dover with his finger pointing toward the aerial vehicle.

Turning quickly, Dover had also realized that Philips was not in his presence. He too had assumed, but in the opposite way.

"I figured that you might want to see something else. You seem relatively bored with these vehicles," Dover claimed.

"Well, shouldn't I learn how to operate and fix this one?" Philips asked, pointing to the aerial vehicle.

The two had been calling out to each other. Narrowing the gap between them, Philips made his way towards Dover. While Dover, on the other hand, stood still waiting for Philips to catch up to him. It did not take long for Philips to reach him as the two now stood just feet from one another.

"What, the Hawk? Can you fly a gravity helicopter?" Dover was referring to a standard military vehicle.

"Yes, I can." Philips flaunted.

"Can you fix one?"

"Yes, but that has thruster on it."

"Hell, if those break down, chances are the thing can't be fixed."

He could not tell whether Dover was joking or not so he simply disregarded the so-called *Hawk* and walked with him. There must have been something extremely interesting that Dover wanted to show him that he would just throw aside preparing Philips for his job. The two walked out of the ordinance room's exit and entered the intricate hallway system that Philips had become so accustom to. He watched Dover pull his flat hand held device from his underarm and turn it on. The device gave off the same blue illumination that was present with the screen in the G.U.V. With a few flicks of his wrist and touches with his fingers, Avi appeared before them once again.

"So where are we going?" Philips asked.

"We are going to where the magic happens." Dover answered.

"Where the magic happens?"

"He means my insides," Avi stated.

"Your insides?" Philips directed toward Avi, becoming slightly irritated with the confusion of their circular game.

Avi and Dover chuckled together.

"We are going to Avi's core. It is called the nuclear room, but it is essentially her heart. It is what keeps her running."

Feeling overwhelmed, Philips asked, "So why am I the one being shown all this?"

Philips had asked the question before he had recognized that Dover had stopped in front of a normal-sized door. The door parted for the three and Dover led the way into the room with Avi in his hand. Philips stepped into the room as he followed the two. He stopped for a moment, standing just beyond the door and examined the room in the same manner he had with every other. The room was surprisingly small but held a giant cylinder structure in its center. In the cylinder was what seemed to be a form of electrical current flowing wildly with bolts touching all sides. The cylinder reached to the ceiling and was not all that wide. He was weary of getting too close to it, considering that the only thing that separated the uncontrollable bolts from him was the cylinder's glass encasing.

"I am showing you all this because you are our field engineer. And, God forbid, if something happens to me or the colonel, it is up to you to work with Avi. Basically, this is what keeps Avi running," Dover informed.

Complete fabrication, Philips sensed. Yes, he was the engineer responsible for fixing up the vehicles and weapons, but he recognized that the chance of something happening to both individuals was extremely low. Besides, based on what he had learned while sitting in the vehicle, he could simply tell Avi what to do without any technical knowledge of her. This lesson that Dover was giving to Philips was merely an effort of show-and-tell. Still, Philips did not disrespect him for putting on the show; he simply acknowledged that the man took pride in his work.

"So why isn't this room a restricted room?" Philips asked, with the hope of gaining secret information.

"Oh, so I see you have looked into the mapping system we have aboard," Dover said with a brief laugh. "I am not too worried about anybody destroying Avi from this room."

"If one was to destroy my core, they would be destroying themselves." Avi interrupted.

"What do you mean?" Philips questioned.

Dover responded with his eyes fixed on Philips. "What Avi is saying is that if someone were to destroy her core, then the entire ship would detonate. Hence the nuclear room."

Philips studied the cylinder and the ecstatic motion from its inside. *It is hard to believe that there would be such risk aboard the ship*, he thought. *However, it seemed incongruously reassuring in the sense that no one would bother this room because of its detrimental competencies. Even the slightest mistake in this room could be the end of not only the artificial intelligence it runs but every life aboard. In a way, the room was so unsafe that it was safe.*

He looked down at Avi and glared at her blankly for a moment. She returned a stare, but hers was more gentle and comforting. She seemed harmless; however, being that Philips had never worked with an A.I. before, he was unsure towards fully trusting her. He turned away from her and looked back at Dover.

"Avi is relatively powerful then, wouldn't you say?" Philips stated with a sense of trepidation in his eyes. "If something cannot be killed what's stopping it from becoming too powerful."

Dover explained pointing towards the monitor that resided at the base of the cylinder. "We have developed a virus, a computer virus, which would kill her if she ever became corrupt."

"So what does the virus do?"

"Basically, it is administered by typing in the formula into the monitor. Doing so deactivates Avi's functioning. It is safe because it does destroy the nuclear reactor that keeps her running. It simply disables her. The virus's formula can be administered in different parts of Avi's memory to possibly prevent her from accessing different areas on the ship, performing certain functions, and even eliminating certain knowledge of things. Worst case scenario, the formula is inputted into her main hard drive. That would incapacitate her completely."

73

Avi continued to stare at Philips with her calm eyes. "Lieutenant, you can trust me. I have no benefit in the crew's destruction. I am simply part of the crew." She chuckled, "Plus, deactivation is non-beneficial for me."

Philips thought for a moment about what was just said. It was comforting to hear that there was a way to prevent Avi from gaining too much control. Surprisingly, it was actually more comforting to hear Avi assure Philips that she had no intention of uprising. The fact that she labeled herself as a crew member gave Philips the belief that she truly had humanistic qualities. Although he still had his doubts, he would try to trust her to his best ability.

Curiously, Philips wondered and asked, "Who else knows of this computer virus?"

"Colonel Goodwin and I are the only ones who know of it and how to use it," Dover said with subtle confidence in his voice.

In an effort to test Dover's loyalty to Goodwin, Philips schemed up a plan in his head. A plan that consisted of divulging any information Dover might know about the mission's true objective.

"And what of Goodwin?" Philips asked. "Do you trust him to not exploit this knowledge?"

"I don't think there is anything to worry about. Goodwin was there for when I first developed the original R.P.S.E., way before Avi's time. He and I have been working on this project for years."

"Has he told you everything about the mission?"

Dover was slightly confused by the question but proceeded to answer. "He has told me everything that was important. I know as much as everyone else."

The comment stopped the conversation dead in its tracks. Philips wished he had not heard Dover say those last few words as they gave him eerie feeling of discomfort. A man of Dover's importance in the expedition must have known more than the other crew members. It was vital that the person who was responsible for creating and calculating the technical aspects of the expedition knows the most about its objective. Either Dover had known the full intentions of the mission or had been kept from full information. Dover appeared to be a pleasant and caring individual; therefore, Philips concluded that the second possibility was most likely.

There was a pause after Dover's statement that had given him the idea that their conversation had ended. During this pause, Philips had been engrossed in his thought becoming stuck on the possibility of concealed information. Dover noticed that Philips's focus had shifted elsewhere, so he gradually started to make his way to the door.

"Are you okay, Lieutenant?" Dover asked as he backed his way to the door with his eyes fixed on the pondering Philips.

Philips raised his eyes to Dover's level and assured.

"I am fine. Just be watchful. I have a feeling that Colonel Goodwin is up to something."

This moment had been the first time Philips had revealed his suspicion about Goodwin directly to a crew member. Dover's blindness had made him susceptible, and Philips felt it necessary to at the minimum offer a warning. He would hate to see a good man, such as Dover, suffer because of the evils of another.

"I trust Goodwin," Dover said lightly. "This is his mission and I don't think he would do anything to jeopardize it or us. I am sorry the training was so brief," he said sincerely. "We are landing soon so I have to prepare." He furthered noticed the apprehension in Philips's face and attempted to further comfort him. "Lieutenant, don't worry about the colonel, trust me."

Philips intently watched Dover leave the nuclear room. As Dover's back faced Philips, he caught a glimpse of Avi, who was still present upon Dover's device. He noticed Avi glaring at him with a concerned look glazed upon her solid blue pupils. For a moment, Philips felt as though Avi and he had shared the same thought. Their minds seemed to come together and unite as one. Though it was brief, Philips could sense the fear within her.

Her fear could not have come solely from Goodwin's possible intentions. There was something greater that distressed the A.I., something much darker.

AND SO IT BEGINS

Meanwhile, during Dover's generous teachings of the inner workings and innovations of Avi, the colonel and his doctored partner held other plans. Their plans were more along the lines of something humanly questionable. Even though, to this point, the two had kept their secret relatively unknown, they were close to revealing a radical and groundbreaking creation. Something no human had experience before.

Goodwin stood over the left shoulder of Dr. Porter examining his preparations. The two stood in a room that no one else aboard had known about—a room that even Goodwin and Porter had barely touched. It was dark, unlike the quarters and hallways that had been so bright throughout the ship. Standing before them was a table that was poorly lit by a dim cherry-red beam. The light came from a fixture that hung from the ceiling, directly above the table's center. Occasionally, the light would flicker at an on-and-off pace as a strobe light would in a night club.

Feeling the heat that came from the red light, both men began to perspire causing liquid stains across their uniform-covered chests. Oddly, the men were unfazed by the heat of the light and had been infatuated with what manifested before their eyes. Porter's view of the specimen was the clearest considering that Goodwin had to stretch his head significantly over Porter's backside in order to appreciate the chromatic beauty. Realizing this strain, Goodwin shifted to his right so that the men stood side by side, parallel to the table.

"How close are they?" Goodwin asked as he reached out in front of himself, hovering his hand just over the right side specimen's softly rounded shell.

Porter pulled his eyes sight away from the shell before him and glared at Goodwin's hand floating above the other.

"Don't touch it, Colonel!" he exclaimed causing Goodwin to lower his hand to his side.

Porter reverted back to his own egg-like entity and examined its polished outer covering. The egg was round on every angle and became slightly pointed on its top. The red light gave it a pinkish glow mixing with its white encasing. Just below the egg, there was a labeling that showed two words and a one-word description. The label spelled out subject E followed by a colon and the word *female* in its description.

In Porter's hand, he held a long and thin metal tool similar to that of tweezers. With the utensil, he gracefully cleaned the egg of any debris and environmental fragments. Once he had cleared the encasing of any imperfections, he lowered the tweezers to the table releasing them completely. His eyes remained fixed on the object causing his hand to bounce around the table blindly. Feeling around for a moment, he eventually found the device he was in search of. A rectangular screened device met the gentle caress of his hand. The device made its way to the egg sitting over top of it. He touched the screen a few times, and it beeped and rang with automated noises.

"This embryo is growing much faster than I expected," he stated moving to the egg in front of Goodwin. This egg was labeled *Subject A: Male.*

Goodwin moved further to the side allowing Porter to gather his images.

"Good, now we can have them ready sooner."

"Like I said before you cannot rush this process," Porter corrected. "Just because the embryo looks to be growing at a substantial rate does not ensure that it will be ready when we think it is. Remember, we are dealing with a new species here. Besides it seems as if subject E is developing slightly faster than A."

"Is that bad?" Goodwin asked.

"Well it means that there is going to be one before the other," Porter informed as he pointed at the left side.

"That's fine," Goodwin spoke seemingly dejected. "I guess that we could just hold the female in the containment room until the male is born." He placed his hands at his side. "How much of a time separation are you talking?"

"I am not sure." Porter sighed. "It could be minutes or hours. Possibly days of separation between their births. There is no telling when. I might need more time."

"Dr. Porter, we are on a timeline here. Any divergence from the timeline could cause the entire operation to be compromised."

Porter placed his screening device gently on the table avoiding any damage to it. He turned his entire body towards the colonel and glared into his eyes. The two stood a few inches from one another. There had always been a sense of conflict that rested between the two. If it were not for the fact that the two relied on one another to reach their own personal goals, the conflict between them would have been too great to sustain a relationship.

"Damn you, Goodwin! You know that I cannot risk speeding up their birth," Porter said while raising his tone and deepening his voice. Now, recognizing that Goodwin needed Porter in order for the operation to advance, he claimed his upper hand. "You have no say in how this organism is created. I am the one with the ability to create, not you!"

Fire glazed across Goodwin's eyes.

"You seem to forget, Dr. Porter," Goodwin said touching upon each syllable of his name. "You are under a contract."

"I told you before, Colonel Goodwin," Porter said matching the syllable scheme. "I never cared about the money."

Goodwin laughed and grew serious again. "It isn't just the money. Your contract states much more than what you will be paid. You are being funded by the United States government. I could take away this precious project at any time. You don't own the life that you see here."

Goodwin held his index finger aggressively in the direction of the table. The force of the gesture tensely compressing the muscles and flesh of his arm. He had hoped this physical presence would be excessive enough to express the power he held over Porter.

The argument had become more of a stand-off as they both realized the power that they each held over one another. They both felt that their own contributions to the operation were more important than the other.

Settling down slightly, Goodwin lowered his arm and attempted to calm his emotions.

"You will have this ready or our deal is off."

"Stop bluffing, we both know you wouldn't end this mission just because of a meaningless deadline," Porter challenged with a smirk. "You would simply reactivate communications and contact your precious charity fund to give us more money and more time." He digressed briefly, "Yes, don't think I don't know about you hindering our communications. I don't doubt that you'll kill off the crew either. Hell, you are probably going to kill me as well. That is once you get what you need from me."

"The hell with you, Porter, and your accusations!" Goodwin's aggression had returned and had actually reached a point of shouting.

The volume of their dialogue had now peaked so that each word created a sense of discomfort among the counterpart. Their tension was always subtle in their interaction and had never reached a point of shouting. They stood face-to-face with their eyes burning through each other. A witness could have seen steam literally evaporating from their heads and creating a climatic cloud above them.

Goodwin calmed himself and continued.

"You will complete this project in the time that I have given you. Like I said I will end what you created here as well as your funding and any future hope of you creating again. If you cannot do it, then I will find someone who can. This is *my* mission. I am running it under *my* terms."

"I don't care for your money, I don't care for your mission, and hell, I don't care for you. No one can create life like I can. *You* need me and *you* cannot succeed in this mission without *me*," he retorted, mimicking Goodwin's previous statement.

There was a pause between their argument and contest over who held the power in their relationship. It seemed that nether was going to except that both held equal power. The conflict between them was only destined to grow and not diffuse. Although their collaboration could result in great progressions in humanity, it would never equivocate into a friendship. Ego and supremacy were the traits that consumed them so thoroughly that companionship was never truly an option.

Taking a step back, Porter realized that their conversation had gained no progress and was only creating further conflict between them. He did not want to deal with Goodwin anymore so he returned to his research by monitoring subject A. He calmly examined the male egg and cleaned it of the inadequacies that had graced their presence upon the shell. However, Goodwin did not take being ignored lightly.

"I am not sure why I even trust you to do this job," Goodwin complained. "We don't even know if you can create life with your virus… After all, you were too incompetent to save your wife."

The words stung Porter's ears like a wasp. He looked up quickly, violently gripping the tweezers so that stuck out the top of his hand. Turning sharply, he knocked over his screening device shattering it across the floor. With his opposite hand, he wrapped Goodwin's neck and forced his backside up against the wall. Slowly, he raised the tweezers and stopped them at Goodwin's eyelevel. The point of the utensil was held just centimeters from Goodwin's eye.

Porter never dreamed of attacking Goodwin considering that he had a slight disadvantage in size and training. However, a line had been crossed between the two. Goodwin knew what he had said, but he did not mean for it to be an attack on Porter. Simply, it was a slip of the tongue that had put Goodwin in a precarious disposition. Porter's boiling blood had caused the rooms temperature to increase from its already significantly warm climate. Goodwin looked into his face helplessly and was temporarily paralyzed due to the surprise of the attack. From behind Porter the cherry, red light seemed to grow brighter, seizing the overall intensity of the room.

"You don't speak of her ever," said Porter as pushed hard into Goodwin's neck causing the colonel to partially stick to the wall. There he stayed for a moment following the leisurely release. Once the colonel was free, he gathered himself by pulling away from the wall and stood up straight. He placed a hand on his neck and gently rubbed it.

Porter began to speak again. "I will complete this project and everything will go according to plan."

Porter's anger subsided; he understood that Goodwin did not mean to say what he had. However, he was now in hopes of disproving the statement and would not accept failure this time.

"I am sorry," Goodwin apologized, his voice trembling.

"It's fine," Porter returned harshly.

"Just understand that we can't exploit time. Our time in this mission is limited. This has to be finished on time."

"It will," Porter spoke with his punitive tone.

The pulsing intensity of their conversation had settled, but it was officially ended upon the occurrence of a sound above them. Both snapped to attention at the sound's presentation and listened intently. Goodwin looked up to the ceiling where he saw the round speaker that delivered the sound. On the other hand,

Porter returned back to his scientific work while he listened. The waves from the speaker drifted away from just a sound to a sound that carried words. The words then turned into formulated sentences, clearly making the source identifiable.

"Attention crew," Avi addressed. "The ship will be approaching Exodus-117 shortly. Each crew member should report to the cockpit for landing and further instructions by Colonel Goodwin.

The intercom stopped delivering information, and Goodwin took his eyes off of it. He opened his mouth with the intention of speaking to Porter; however, he failed in doing so. His mouth reverted back to its closed position. Porter sensed Goodwin's glare and turned to face him once more.

"Colonel, I believe that is your cue."

Awkwardness filled the air that separated the two. The colonel was still shaken up by the abrupt attack. He had become slightly frightened by the suppressed aggression Porter held within himself. It was not so much the physical fear that Goodwin had, but it was more the fear of the unknown. He made his way to the room's exit. The doors parted and Goodwin was stopped before he crossed into the hallway.

"Oh and Colonel…. Have faith."

LANDING A NEW BEGINNING

"Look at it," Zuckerman exclaimed, standing next to the glass that surrounded the cockpit.

"It looks so much alike," returned Thatcher, who stood next him.

Philips made his way over to their voices in order to catch a better glimpse. He stood to the right of Thatcher and examined the visual that was presented before him. A sense of peace embraced his being while his blood flowed through his body giving him a warm feeling. His hopes and dreams seemed to come together for a moment as he stared at the round sphere. It resembled all the ideas and concepts he so greatly wanted to obtain—a chance to restart and a chance to refresh all the goodness of humanity.

He pulled his eyes from the window and moved them around the cockpit. Everyone, including Goodwin, was absorbed into the beauty that resided just outside their ship. However, Philips believed that it was much more than beauty. By noticing everyone's amazement with the planet, he thought of the potential. Yes, it would be a fresh start and deliverance of human goodness, but it could also be so much more. Something such as this could destroy the inconsistency of man. It could relieve the evils that had plague humanity on Earth. For the first time in a while, Philips had been experiencing a sense of growing belief. Virginity would be its essence—untouched and unscathed by human fallacies.

A hand was placed on his shoulder causing him to find its source. It was the hand of Watkins, who did not look at him, for his eyes were too fixed on the captivating image. Philips smiled at Watkins and copied his same action.

"It's beautiful, isn't it?" Watkins asked.

"Yeah, it is," Philips answered.

The sphere before them was certainly earth-like from its outside appearance. Space was clear showing a profusion of micro-gas balls dancing around the planet like an ancient tribe around a fire. Among the smaller stars was their leader, an enlarged mass of orange-yellow heat that was the size of Exodus multiplied a few times. The giant mass was bright and directly angled towards the planet and at the sides of Exodus were two surrounding grey rocks. The rocks taunted the planet from both sides, but the planet seemed unaffected with its considerably larger size. The moons, at the moment, avoided Exodus's path of visibility to its source of light. However, this light must have been partial, Philips assumed, as he noticed that a blanket of moisture produced the grey that had dispersed its way around the planet. Philips could see only few parts of the planet's topography where the landscape was covered by either masses of blue or grey.

"I didn't bring my bathing suit, Colonel Goodwin," Rodriguez sardonically said. Rodriguez stood toward the front of the cockpit relatively close to the colonel. "I hope this ship can float on water because it looks like we'll be swimming."

Goodwin, who seemed to have forgotten about his scuffle with Porter, grinned and spoke. "Regrettably, the ship doesn't float. That being said, we are going to have to find a dry spot to land." He moved away from the window and made himself a comfortable standing place where he stood during lift off. "Seats everyone," he commanded.

The crew headed to the seating section. Philips found his seat from before and watched as everyone matched their earlier placements. Once everyone had situated themselves in a comfortable and relaxed position, they gave their attention to Goodwin.

"Congratulations crew," he began. "You all are about to become the first men…" he looked at Rodriguez, "…and women," then returned to the entire crew, "to step foot on this miraculous planet, Exodus. We are now just above its atmosphere, and it is time for your vacations to end. When we land our contracts are all fully in affect." His voice grew stern. "If anyone fails to comply with their contractual obligations, they will be dismissed from my crew. Is that understood?"

Those among the seated nodded their heads. Philips, in the midst of a head nod, noticed that Dr. Porter was not present in the cockpit. Everyone aboard the ship arrived except for the lead scientist of the expedition. The colonel preached before them, Mr. Dover worked behind Goodwin with Avi and his prized screens, and the rest of Goodwin's working grunts were amidst the seats. It was somewhat ironic for the scientific leader aboard to be absent during their detailed job descriptions.

"Good," the colonel acknowledged. "As you all can see this planet is very much like Earth."

He turned to the screen that separated him from Dover and the lower front of the cockpit. The screen was large and stretched the length of the seated section. With the hand motions that had become so recurring, he spun his wrist and twiddled his fingers. Images displayed on the screen swiftly pirouetted and glided from all its angles. Finally, he motioned his hand and fingers in the correct way, exposing different images of the planet. The images had been broken up into different sizes and outlooks of Exodus. He kept his arm up in the air so that he could play with the images while he faced the crew.

"Yes, it has a star that is measured to be similar in distance from that of our sun and Earth. This means that it too acts like our sun, heating and lightening this planet. On the other hand, it differs in a few ways. I am sure that you noticed the two rocky spheres floating around Exodus. Those are its moons," Goodwin's tone held a mundane and mocking tone. "They revolve Exodus, have the same rotation speed, and conveniently reside across from each other. The other alteration is that Exodus sits almost perfectly with about a two-degree tilt."

"—So I am assuming that the planet has no seasons. Just consistent weather." Rodriguez stopped Goodwin.

Goodwin drew his hand down the planet's core.

"That is what we we're assuming as well. And this is where your jobs start to come into play." He looked at Rodriguez and Zuckerman. "You two will be responsible for analyzing and recording the atmospheric and geographical aspects of Exodus. I want to know the temperature, the pressure, the water content, the weather patterns, everything and anything that you deem necessary for livability." He pointed his finger and bounced it up and down as he spoke. "You will report to me anything that you believe is questionable. I want accurate readings. If something is a hair of figure off, then you will report it to me. Understood?"

The two earth scientists nodded to show their compliance.

"Dr. Thatcher," Goodwin addressed, looking in Thatcher's direction. "Do what you do best and give us the readings on the physics of the planet. Obviously if the crew is floating with each step, then we would know it is different than Earth. But, I want you to gather data on gravitational forces and any other physical effects of the planet."

Goodwin began to walk the length of the screen back and forth. His hands were placed behind his back, one holding the other. With his head held high, he moved one foot in front of the other continuously. When he would reach the end of the screen, he would rotate his footing and begin in the opposite direction.

Finally he spoke again. "Now, weapons and repair," he began. "Corporal Daniels, Sergeant Watkins, and Lieutenant Philips, hopefully we won't need the usage of any one of you."

"So our vacation continues," Watkins said casually.

Daniels and Philips sat quietly but smiled briefly at Goodwin's aim. Without stopping his walking pace, the colonel also scarcely smiled.

"Nothing personal, Sergeant. I would just rather avoid any violence and equipment malfunctioning. However, if the situation presents itself in either way, then you three will be expected to do your jobs. I will be pairing you with the scientists during the planet's inspection. Make sure nothing gets in the way of their studies."

Philips watched Dover move behind Goodwin and around to the front of the visual screen. He stood at its end and looked at Goodwin. He waited for him to finish debriefing and gave him eye contact. Once Goodwin had noticed the eyes of the crew drift toward Dover's direction, he did the same.

"Are we ready?" Goodwin asked.

"Yes sir." Dover nodded and leered.

"All right, lead us into history books, Mr. Dover."

"Avi, set ship for landing," Dover ordered. "Let's make this nice and smooth."

"Ship set for landing," Avi returned. "Reversing thrusters and reducing impact speed."

A traceable sound came from the windows of the cockpit. Philips witnessed space disappeared at the sound of gears grinding and metal covering the visual. The layering of the metal blanket moved around the glass covering almost all of the surrounding entirely. The clanking of metal stopped just at the front windshield-like part of the ship, enabling the crew and, most importantly, the pilots to see the atmosphere they entered. Dover and Goodwin now found their seats and strapped in, just as the other members had already done. Following the action, an immediate sense of forces began to grow. Upon this notification, Philips gripped intensely on his armrests.

"Eighty-five percent," Avi informed.

"S-slow us d-down Avi," Dover shouted.

Philips kept his eyes forward on the windshield as the planet became gradually bigger and bigger. Pockets and strips of grey, floating vapor smacked the front of the ship without making a sound. The ship ripped through clouds like melting butter, but the easiness of the ship's slicing had caused somewhat of a panic.

"Sixty-five percent," Avi stated.

"Damn it Dover, we are coming in too fast!" Goodwin yelled focusing on him.

Dover seemed to ignore Goodwin and stared straight through the atmosphere. "More forward thrust Avi"

"Forty percent," Avi said again. "Forward thrusters are at a maximum speed."

Even without any knowledge of how the ship ran, Philips had become frightened with the fact that he could see the ground of the planet. Their speed was too great for the distance left in their landing. His head was glued to the headrest and his mind was stuck on the fear of death by crashing. The ship's nose was pointed to the ground and the crew's new destination had seemed to change to the core of Exodus.

"Handle the situation, Mr. Dover," Goodwin said with an unforeseen and mutable tone.

"Twenty-five percent."

Their crash was seemingly imminent; conversely, Dover had a trick up his sleeve. "Avi hit the mid-thrust now!"

The ship came to a quick but suave stop with just a few yards from the planet's surface. It began to hover in a valley that stretched a few miles before it was met by water. Philips sighed with relief and placed his hand on his chest. His heart prodded from his chest immensely while his head was wrapped around a thought of disbelief. He continued to watch the windshield thriller come to an epic conclusion as the ship had leveled itself out horizontally. The event forced his view away from the rocky ground of the planet and to its horizon. Even though the ship sat lower than the cliff ledges surrounding it, it was distantly safe from the potential of any flooding. The land around them was lifeless and covered with rocks and weathered stones. Grey was the valley's chosen color theme and elicited the concept that the crew would have to travel outside of it in order to find life and vegetation.

At the sight of the sky, his mind enchantingly drifted from the thought of death to beauty. Though it was a cloudy mural, he could barely see Exodus's sun shining through the atmospheric covering. It began to slowly fade away until he could no longer see its shine and the area surrounding was filled with darkness. The ship landed aggressively causing him to vibrate in his seat. Nevertheless, the harsh thrust from the ground was a mere distraction for his temporary focus. He had become caught up in the splendor of Exodus's transition from day to night.

"Well," Goodwin said, standing from his seat and matriculating to the front of the crew. "It would seem that we landed at the start of night. I guess this means the expedition will have to wait until morning."

Philips could sense the disappointment in Goodwin's voice. But, he was not the only person who was geared toward instant discovery. From the looks of the rest of the crew, everyone seemed slightly discontent of the minor setback.

Dover spoke over Goodwin. "Avi, what is the sunrise time."

"Approximate sunrise time from my readings are zero six hundred," Avi answered. "In Earth time, of course."

"You heard her," Goodwin stated to the crew. "0600, so I suggest you all get some rest. Tomorrow, we begin."

Those were the final words that Philips heard from anyone for the rest of the night. He trudged himself through the ship and to his room with no further interaction or contact from anyone. Once he arrived to his room, he attempted to contact his wife and son; however, the connection still remained down. It was not as discouraging as it had been originally, simply because he had grown accustom to the distance that had grown between them. Therefore, he was stuck with the three words, "tomorrow we begin."

He lied perfectly still with his back to his tightly sprung mattress, eyes on the room's ceiling. Mixed feelings raced through his mind, each competing for a spot in his immediate train of thought. His thoughts ranged from the exploration and excitement tomorrow held to the family he had left behind to the hope he so desperately wanted. Still, no matter what thought he had it always seemed to lead to him thinking of Dr. Nar Porter. The first few thoughts he resisted its urge, but after a while he caved into granting Porter the right to rule his mind.

It started with the simple question of why Dr. Porter was not present in the cockpit for landing. Where was he? Was he still aboard? What was he doing? His mind was rampant with questions that he knew he could most likely not answer. Even the ceiling above him had morphed from its white base to a colorful painting. A painting that shaped itself into a head that had fair skin and hair. He stared at it as it stared back with dark eyes. They pierced deeply into his soul, seeming to grab it from within himself and rip it clean from his body.

GENESIS OF A PLANET

Tersely, Philips awoke in a cold-sweat to a ship-wide alarm system. Avi's humdrum tone informed the crew that they had fifteen minutes to eat and meet in the ship's bay before departure. Philips sat up and wiped the perspiration from his forehead. The neck of his uniform was damp causing him to look down and examine the discomfort. As he looked down, he saw a wooden object poking through the top part of his tightly gripped fist. He opened his hand and laid his palm flat. There the object sat in the middle of his hand with its make up consisting of two disproportionate sticks intersecting through each other. He was confused of how it found its way from his pocket to his hand, so he discerned that he was only having a nightmare.

He rolled himself out of the bed and placed the cross on a bedside table. After he stood up and stretched himself into a fully awakened state, he walked over to the laundry machine that resided inside the walled closet. As he pressed the center button, the doors of the closet-like machine opened and displayed his uniforms. He grabbed a new uniform set and quickly pushed into the spandex material. Without much thought, he routinely swiped the cross from the table and placed it in his pocket as he slid on his shoes.

His hunger was not prodigious in the least bit, so he skipped breakfast and head directly to the bay. Other than him briefly reflecting on his nightmare, the morning had been absent of any thought of Dr. Porter. Instead, his eagerness of expedition occupied his concentration. He walked through the ship at a quicker pace than usual, seeing that his anticipation fueled him like adrenaline. It took him a few minutes to reach the bay; however, once he arrived he realized he was not the only one who was eager. In fact, he was one of the last to reach the bay.

"Man, I guess no one was hungry," said Watkins.

The crew laughed as Dover directed everyone to the equipment room that was another closet-like room within the ship.

"No, Sergeant. We are just hungry for planetary investigation," Thatcher exclaimed as he patted Watkins on the back. Watkins looked over his shoulder in his direction and bobbed with a smirk.

"I guess so, Dr. Thatcher. I guess so." Watkins replied.

As Dover exposed the secret room, Philips caught a glimpse of their outdoor uniform for the first time. His eyes touched upon each facet of the uniform while Dover handed out its pieces. The uniform came in two parts: the first part was the helmet and the second was the body suit. Dover first handed out a body suit to each departing member. The suit was hardly malleable, almost giving it the ability to stand alone. Philips felt its exterior and it recognized that its material was firm. When each member had a suit before them, Dover instructed by using Zuckerman's suit as an example. He pressed a button near the back of the neck that triggered a response. This response led to a partial opening in the back, which allowed for each member to step into their own.

Philips, following the procedure, moved and flexed his limbs and muscles. The suit was lightly weighed on his body despite its heavy appearance. Philips accredited its weight to the material. Truly, the Kevlar-like material only made up some portions of it, giving it the mien of armor in the parts it covered. What organized the entire suit was a material that was foreign to Philips, but it looked as if it were a thicker form of his ship uniform. Nevertheless, he was indifferent towards the design of body suit and more concerned with it doing its function.

The helmet was the next and last part of the suit's assembly. It was amusing and comically entertaining for Philips to watch the scientist look at their helmets. To the military personal, the helmet seemed familiar to what they had used in combat on Earth. Each of the three had their helmets on before the scientist even realized what they were holding. With a button press in the back of their helmets and a placement on their heads, the helmets hissed and depressurized fully to their body suits. As Dover instructed the helpless, Philips explored the design. It was similar, yet this helmet had a more technologically advanced vibe. From his view in the inside, it had a diagram screen that acted like his own centralized computer, giving him everything from pressure levels to a zooming effect.

He looked through the words and diagrams that displayed in front of his face and at the others who had had their suit fully together. He detected that the characters presented in a person's helmet were subject to that individual. As he observed Daniels' face, all he saw was a clear visor that was shaped like a grin. There were no words or images exhibited on the outside, only on the inside.

For the most part, Philips had been impressed with the sleekness and finery of the technologically advanced space suits. He had honestly thought that the crew was destined to wear something more of a fish bowl for a helmet and a bulky, unmovable white base. In reality, he was keen towards nearly every aspect of its design: its white shade was not too flashy and its tools were vastly innovative.

Dover spoke drawing their attention.

"As you all can see, you have visuals before your eyes that display analysis and other applications. These are each programmed for your job description."

Philips looked to his right towards Rodriguez and noticed her name was written on the side of her helmet.

"These suits have a built-in system that connects with Avi and the communication back to the ship."

Goodwin made a surprise appearance from behind a grounded hawk.

"Mr. Dover and I will be on the ship during your investigation. You will be able to communicate with us while we remain aboard."

He stopped next to Dover and gave him a permissive acknowledgement to speak.

"Lieutenant Philips will be responsible for guiding you through your travels on the planet," Dover said without looking at him.

Goodwin interrupted, "he is your overseer while the crew explores, making him in charge."

The comment did not sit well with Daniels as he let out an evident sigh. Seeing that he held a higher ambition for leadership, there was no misunderstanding why he was perturbed by the colonel's order. However, the sigh was not enhanced by Daniels' disposition, but rather the breathing apparatus that attached to the bottom of the helmet. This source of their oxygen had, in fact, caused all those suited to breathe prominently louder.

The colonel ignored Daniels' childish response to his order and continued to speak.

"Following your return, we will meet once more for further collective group analysis."

"Everyone, let's load up," Dover said.

Philips was soon to be in command of the operation outside the ship, yet he walked in the middle of the pack as they made their way to where the vehicles were located. As they walked, he made the connection that Porter was not at the landing debriefing because he would not be exploring the planet with them. Still, he found it weird that the top scientist aboard the ship was not interested in analyzing a virgin planet.

"Considering our location in terms of water bodies, flying is our only option."

Philips's previous thought faded quickly to a new one. He now apprehended that they were not going to be driving but flying. Philips grew anxious at the thought because he did not even enter the Hawk during his training with Dover. Even though Dover had told him that he would be able to base it on his past experience, it still remained an alien vehicle to him. It was an incident that was likely to give him insecurity.

Once they approached the Hawk, everyone began to enter through its vertically opening doors. The three scientists and Daniels sat in the rear, while Watkins made himself a spot in the passenger's seat. Philips paused before he entered the aerial vehicle, with his hand on the door handle. He glanced at Dover who in return recognized his anxiety, but did not ease it.

"Make sure you land it in a safe grounded area for analysis. These things don't float well." He changed his subject quickly, "Weapons are in the back. I will be in touch."

Dover began to walk away, but stopped and swiveled his head and body in search of his boss. He looked toward the back of the Hawk and spotted two feet below the left-side thruster. The body was not visible due to its vicinity in relation to the thruster. Knowing that the feet belonged to the colonel, Dover passed by the side of the craft and to its rear.

"Colonel, the crew is all set," Dover addressed.

Goodwin pulled his eyes away from the thruster that he had been so visually occupied with.

"Good. Good," he said.

"Shall we make our way to the cockpit?"

Goodwin ignored the question.

"Mr. Dover, are you sure that you wouldn't rather travel with them?"

"I would, but if I go then no one would be here to monitor their connection with Avi"

"I could operate it."

"If it's not too much trouble, I would feel more comfortable staying on board."

The colonel expressed no emotion.

"Understandable. Feel free to make your way to the cockpit now. I would just like to have a few words with the crew."

"Very good sir," Dover concluded as he backed away.

During the conversation, Philips stood outside his pilot's seat with the door opened above his head. He waited as if he expected to hear one last departing word from Dover. As Dover passed him, he merely gave him a pat on the shoulder. Without a final word, Dover was gone. He turned his vision to the rear where he saw Dover's same sighting from before. The feet stayed in place underneath the thruster, but Philips questioned why. Brusquely, Goodwin popped his body away from the rear. Philips hopped into the vehicle, pretending to not have been sneaking a glance at Goodwin. He settled himself in his seat and acted as if he were examining the flight controls.

With his head angled to an unrecognizable degree, he caught a glimpse of Goodwin leaving through his peripherals. Via switch, Philips closed his side door attracting Goodwin to look back to give a solid salute to the vehicle. He hoped Goodwin had not seen him gawking, but the thought did not overly concern him seeing that Goodwin's withdrawal was complete.

A moment of silence allowed Philips to become familiar with the craft he had skipped during training. Dover was not lying to him, for the controls were almost identical to the vehicles he had been accustom to before the expedition. He dialed in a few touches on the center control panel which caused a loud explosive firing from the rear. It was apparent that the engine had ignited and was ready for deployment into the mysterious planet's atmosphere. Following the sound, Avi face illuminated the faces of the others.

"Testing full connection and final transport status. All is good." She said disappearing and taking the illumination with her.

"Can you hear me?" Dover asked.

The voice came from inside the helmets of the crew members. "Loud and clear, Dover," Philips replied.

"Okay, opening the bay doors in five, four, three, two, doors opening. Mission is on you, Lieutenant. Take it away."

The bay door was large, almost like a giant garage door that opened from side to side. It appeared to be two-stories high and about a house length. The sound of the doors opening was absence, or at least it seemed so. For the sound of the Hawk's thruster's had drown any opposing sound. All Philips could hear was a fiery growling that must have ranged throughout the entire bay and onto the new exposed planet. The sound was due to grow considering that Philips pulled back on the hand controls causing the craft to shoot its way passed the opening.

Their speed was by no means overwhelmingly forceful like the launch and landing. It was smooth and agile. Philips rotated and pulled on the controls giving him the maneuverability he desired. The ship flew through the planet's grey atmosphere leaving a slowly growing tail in the sky. In a way, the sound effects that came from the Hawk were similar to what Philips thought it would sound like to have an electric muscle car. In other words, it was loud and relatively automated.

"*New Sumeria*, we are in the air," Philips stated, examining the Hawk's evaluations . "Flight feels the same, atmospheric pressure readings are similar, everything seems normal."

Philips spoke to Dover as he now moved his visual study to the planet itself. Below the craft were masses of dark, deep blue that aquatically jolted around to the air that blew it. There were miles and miles of endless areas of water encumbering Philips's ability to decipher whether it was ocean, lake, or some other form of maritime body. Despite the amount of area the planet's water encompassed, he was able to differentiate where the sky and water separated. It was hard to tell at first with the sky foggily mashing itself with the watered lower half, but during their travels the fog began to subside.

"Copy that, Lieutenant," Dover returned from *New Sumeria*'s cockpit. "What do you see so far?"

"It was partly foggy, but now it is cleared up into somewhat of an overcast sky. We have been flying over water for a while now," Philips answered.

"Do you see any land?"

"Not anything other than what we landed on." Subsequently, he distinguished something growing off in the distance. "Check that, I think we found some. I think my helmets getting a reading of dry land."

As he spoke to Dover, his visor zoomed in toward the land mass ahead presenting topography that was further grey rock. He would not settle for simply another region of gravel, so he continued to look harder. His determination slowly began to fade to extinction until there was a complete reversal in his fortune. Shades of luscious, dark-green filled his visor giving him a sense of renewal. At the sense, he pulled back on the controls causing the craft to gently come to a stop. The chopper lowered to the ground just slightly passed the body of water and in between the green bristle. As it landed, it kicked up pieces of wet debris throwing it into the air.

"Dover, we found a region," Philips said.

He removed his harness and prepared himself. As he turned off the vehicle, he gathered all the energy and courage he needed to exit.

Following the door's raising, his feet hit the rocks. He did not float; he did not fly. In no way did he feel weightless. Taking a few steps out onto the planet's course surface, he spun his head and sight leisurely. Everyone else had either already done this process or was in the midst of doing so. Philips found the forest that had motivated his landing and observed it with purpose. Green had now become one of the planet's new color themes thanks to the vegetation. There were trees that held spruce and pine. With very little space between the trees, Philips saw few exotically colored flowers and boundless amounts of what looked as though it were grass. Appreciating this creative undergrowth, he traced the trails and patches of the grass all the way to where he stood with the crew.

"We landed just past the water and before what appears to be a forest."

"Any life?" Dover asked.

"We haven't seen anything yet, but I will have the scientist run a few tests. Dr. Rodriguez, Dr. Zuckerman." Philips called out as he whirled in search of them.

"Yes Lieutenant," Dr. Rodriguez said revealing himself.

"What are the atmospheric readings?"

"I am running a test right now," Rodriguez said causing the crew to pause for a moment. "It's almost entirely made up of nitrogen. The rest is roughly between nineteen- and twenty-two-percent oxygen."

"Any deadly gases?"

"There is some argon, helium, methane, and others, but no—there is nothing harmful. It seems pretty much breathable."

"Dover can you hear that?"

Dover, being able to hear each crew member, responded.

"Copy that Lieutenant. But keep your helmets on before we run any official tests. We don't want to risk anything yet."

"Agreed. Dr. Thatcher." Philips shouted and looked for the intended individual.

"Lieutenant?"

Philips found him.

"Physical analysis?"

"Yeah, I have been examining and everything is in exact accordance with Earth." He stared at Philips with big eyes. "It's remarkable."

On the ship, Goodwin sat in the cockpit's chairs and listened to the interaction that was spreading throughout the crew. He sat with one leg crossed over the other and his hands out in front of him. His elbows rested against his side, but he pointed his forearms upward. Connecting his arms with his hands, as they met by touching the opposite finger tips. He was completely tranquil and fixed his eyes on Dover while he played with the data and information that the crew was feeding him. His eyes never moved from the busy individual. He just stared at him blankly and kept silent.

Philips could sense the air in a way, even though he was not physically touching Exodus's atmosphere. Just by its appearance he could tell that its temperature was mild, but on the cool side. He inspected the opposite side of the data on his visor. Its outside was lightly wetted enabling Philips to recognize that the overcast sky was releasing small misting droplets of water.

Philips turned back to Rodriguez. "Rodriguez, what is the temperature right now?"

"Fourteen point one degree Celsius," she answered.

He did not respond, considering that he had already mentally guessed a similar number. Instead he walked over to the Hawk and found three rifles from its rear interior. Then he tossed one to Watkins and one to Daniels, leaving one for himself. Daniels cocked the gun and it retorted with a snap.

"Where to now?" Daniels said with a gleaming scowl. "…Sir."

He was obviously still irritated by the leadership choice.

Philips came towards his crew, front of the rifle resting on his shoulder. "Thatcher, Zuckerman, you stay here. Thatcher, I want you to run any further physical diagnosis you need right here in this rocky region. Zuckerman, I want you to analyze this body here." He pointed his finger at the giant water mass. "Find the marine life, if any, and give me the element make-up so we know if we can swim in it, drink it, whatever. And Daniels, be their guardian. Rodriguez and Watkins, we are going to go into the forest ahead and inspect it deeply."

The crew nodded with compliance and they branched out into their mandated groups.

"Dover, I am heading towards the forested region with Dr. Rodriguez and Sergeant Watkins. Thatcher, Zuckerman, and Daniels are staying back to analyze the water and physics. Standby." Philips's excitement grew quickly.

"Copy that." Dover was concerned with their mysterious venture into the forest. "Stay alert."

"Stayin' frosty," Watkins butted in.

As they approached the green pines, a breeze increased. The breeze was not significant, but it was strong enough to kick the spruce onto Philips's visor. With his hand, he reached up and wiped the wetted pieces from the glass. The gun, in his opposing hand, aimed low to the ground, yet his finger kept the trigger ready for any threat.

"What do you see Rodriguez?" Philips's excitement was now mixed with anxiety.

She stared straight. Her head was motionless.

"Boreal."

"Doctor?"

"Sorry. I was saying that this is a Boreal forest."

"As in biomes?"

"Correct."

Philips redirected his attention to Watkins. "How about you D.J.? You picking up any life form."

Watkins gazed at his screen's presentation of a disorganized rainbow. He and Daniels were the only two of the exploration that had thermal vision equipped in their helmets.

"Nothing really," Watkins said. "Mostly living colors, but nothing moving. All I see are plants."

The three entered the forest with subtle nervousness. The accompaniment of each other had halted most of the discomfort, but there was still some lurking. Each step, in the forest, was answered by a stick crackling. Philips looked to the undergrowth and saw miles of fallen spruce. Every angle and viewpoint was consistent. There was either an image of evergreen, prickling trees or a stick consumed ground.

Rodriguez stopped abruptly causing the others to do the same.

"Rodriguez?" Philips was confused by her stoppage.

"Hang on," she responded as she bent down. "I want to take a sample of these flowers."

"Careful Rodriguez, you don't know if it is poisonous or not."

"We will never know unless we find out," Watkins joined in, bending to the side of Rodriguez.

Philips proceeded to do as the others. Watkins did have a valid point and he was grateful for it. If it were not for the comment, Philips would have most-likely continued to walk. However, now having seen the beauty before him, he knew he would have regretted that decision. The flower was small in size, but its array of colors could have lightened even the darkest of times. Rodriguez pulled an unseen tool from her waist. It had a size and shape similar to a flashlight. She held it to the flower and received a visual message from her visor. She stood from her position and the other two followed.

"Flowers, simple yet hold so much elegance in life." She was enlightened. "Isn't that the truth?"

They sustained their journey deeper into the wilderness. They saw more vegetation as the day progressed. Most of what they saw was the continuous pine, but they also found more flowers. It's flora and shrubbery was similar to Earth is so many ways. After a while, Philips realized that the group had been walking through the seemingly endless forest for hours. He looked to the sky and saw the clouds begin to part. The sky undressed itself steadily, baring its naked blue. For the third time, Philips saw Exodus's sun. It was brighter than ever. Off to its side was one of the two moons of Exodus. He followed its progression as well. It too was brighter than ever and continued to grow brighter as the sun faded into the evening. Exodus was revised so that the sun brightened the day and the moons illuminated the night.

As dusk caused the sun to kiss the horizon, Philips and his accompanies were awoken from their dream-state. He knew that their best chance at a safe return was while they still had daylight. His recognition was followed by connection with the ship.

"Dover, Avi," he called. "How much daylight is left?"

"According to Avi, you have a few hours. You might want to start thinking about packing it in for the day and gathering the rest of your data for post analysis."

"Copy that Dover." Philips spoke as he spun his finger in a circular motion. His escorts understood the gesture and reversed their course. "On our way back."

Philips changed his frequency to Zuckerman.

"Come in Zuckerman," Philips requested.

"Go ahead, Philips." Zuckerman responded.

"We are headed back now. Any luck with the water analysis?"

"Yes sir. We ran a few tests and each one showed that this mass we landed next to is a basic fresh hydrogen oxide system. Almost like a giant lake of some sort. But that's not the best part." He hesitated in order to build Philips's anticipation. "The water and air both have life."

"Life?" Philips's eyes grew large at the statement. "Like what?"

"Well, we aren't entirely sure what they are, but we have seen some small creatures in the water and some winged in the air. Like fish and birds."

"Dover, please tell me you heard that," Philips said shifting his frequency back to the *New Sumeria*.

"Loud and clear, Lieutenant," Dover accredited.

They focused back to their return. Though Philips was directing his group, he was also in thought. He had grown pleased with the idea that there was life on the planet, but he still remained unconvinced. Maybe it was the fact that he had not seen the life for himself. Granted, the discovery of the planet's foliage was a remarkable feat in itself, yet he desired to see the creatures that benefited from it. He remained patient and would soon be rewarded.

Their walk had been caught between a stroll and a jog. The sun was setting fast and the last thing Philips wanted was the crew to be stuck on a dark and unknown planet. The clouds had begun to make their way back into the sky's scenic picture. Rain began to fall gently, but did not hinder their return in the least bit.

"Where are we?" Rodriguez had become irritated by the wet conditions.

"We are close," Philips reassured. "Half a kilometer from the—"

Both Philips and Watkins stopped and held their rifles pointed ahead of them. Rodriguez was startled by the action, but froze as well. The butts of the rifles were jammed harshly into their shoulders. Philips peered down and through his scope at a moving object a few yards ahead.

"What is it?" Watkins whispered.

Phillips blinked and moved his neck back and forth. He squinted his aiming eye by raising his cheek. The object moved through a colorful group of flowers graciously. It was small but clear through a scope.

"What do you guys see?" Rodriguez was not able to see it because she lacked a rifle.

"A life form," Philips answered.

Philips took a step forward with one foot only. The groundcover crackled at the pressure of his foot causing the creature to look up at him. He had a perfect visual of it now. It had become immobilized at the sound of Philips's step; however, it returned to its previous activities after a few seconds. It was grey—like the planet—and had short legs, giving it a low center of gravity. The species had a long head, ears, and tail for its body size. Philips experiences on Earth yielded him the idea that it was something similar to a terrier-sized rat.

He shared his sightings with the others. "It's definitely a species of some sort. Kind of like a large rat."

"Does it look threatening?" Rodriguez wanted to ensure her safety.

"I doubt it," Watkins comforted.

Watkins undoubtedly saw the creature as Philips did. It was harmless. It nibbled on one patch of flowers and then hoped to the next. Rodriguez wanted to catch a glimpse of the species so she walked towards it slowly. The two soldiers lowered their weapons, for Rodriguez's aggressive approach resulted in scaring it away.

That spotting was the last of their journey into the forest as they exited the spruce shortly after. There was still some partial daylight once they reached the others and the Hawk, enough to fly them back safely. As the crew gathered together inside the Hawk, they shared the data and stories they had experienced throughout the day. Philips pressed the buttons that had started the aerial vehicle before, but this time he did not share the same luck. He repeated the process and again the engine started and stalled. The sound had stopped the crew's collaboration and turned their focus to Philips and the ship.

"Having problems, Lieutenant Philips," said Daniels and the first person to comment considering his envy.

"I don't know to be honest. This is how it started before and it flew fine," Philips said.

"Systems are probably down." Watkins showed support.

"Yeah. Exodus to *New Sumeria*." Philips phoned Dover one last time.

"Yes, Lieutenant," Dover responded.

"Um, well, we have somewhat of a dilemma here. Can you connect me to Avi so she can take a look at the system? The Hawk seems to be malfunctioning."

Back on *New Sumeria*, Goodwin sat in the same position he had been in all day. Other than the occasional stretch, he had not moved from his seat. It was almost as if he were waiting on something. He stared at Dover, watching his every motion closely.

"Is everything okay Mr. Dover," Goodwin said with a sense of dramatic irony.

"Something seems to be malfunctioning with their flight vehicle." Dover did not look at Goodwin and stayed fixated on his screens. "I am transferring Avi to them now to see if she can diagnosis and fix it."

Avi's illumination had returned to the Hawk once more and so had the crews blue faces. She looked downward, almost like she was working on an actual entity before her. In a way, Philips assumed this action was for the purpose of artificial intelligence animation.

"From my diagnosis," Avi stated looking at Philips, "I can fix this."

"Great," Philips exclaimed.

"Only down side is that the repair would take ten hours." She was cavalier.

"Ten hours? What are our options here, Dover?"

Dover took a moment to think. "Well, we could have you wait it out while Avi repairs the failure."

"No," Goodwin said to Dover. Dover was the only person to hear him. "I will not have the crew stuck out there for ten hours in the dark. This is a foreign planet and we know very little right now. I want them back here as soon as possible." Goodwin was lying through his teeth. His true motive was different yet hidden.

Dover paused his connection with the crew and spoke toward Goodwin.

"What do you expect to happen then? That is the only plausible solution."

"You will fly out there and get them."

"And simply leave a piece of equipment that is millions of dollars. You said it yourself, we know little about this planet. Something could happen to the Hawk." Dover was frustrated with Goodwin's simple resolution.

"Dover," Goodwin held his death stare. "I am not asking. That's an order."

Dover became discouraged with his temporary lack of authority. He thought the decision was extremely controversial being that he was in charge of the equipment and technology aboard the ship. He did not need any more heat than he was most-likely going to receive upon their arrival back to Earth. The loss of connection with Earth would later be a problem that would be taken up by the government. Dover was the easiest one to blame for anything technology based.

He reconnected with the crew on Exodus and continued to trade a stare with Goodwin.

"Philips?"

"Yes."

"Change of plans. I will be flying another Hawk to escort you and the crew back. We will leave the other one for now." He cringed at himself saying those words.

"Copy. I am transferring you a map of our location for evac."

Philips touched the side of his helmet sending a topographical display to the cockpit of *New Sumeria*. Dover disconnected a final time and spoke to Goodwin.

"Will you be staying here?"

Goodwin smiled and answered, "Someone has to stay onboard."

THE STORIES ONE SHOULD KNOW

Despite the slowly drizzling sky and the growing darkness, the crew stood just outside of the Hawk. It had become an elongated anticipation waiting for Dover to arrive in a replacement vehicle. Philips grew tired of standing and could feel the fatigued pressure on his thighs, calves, and feet. He made his way over to a large boulder that reside a few yards from the rest of the crew and sat. Though it was firm, Philips hardly noticed its texture with the relief he gained from sitting. He stuck the nose of his rifle into the ground and leaned his layered arms against the butt. A sigh slipped from his lungs and he let his helmet blocked forehead rest on his forearms. From this position, he gradually closed his eyes and escaped from all reality. Peace and tranquility flowed through his body as he embraced the precious images gained from the beautiful planet.

"Christian, you all right?"

Philips removed his forehead and saw Watkins.

"Yeah, I am fine," Philips replied.

"I'll tell you what, Dover better get here soon because my oxygen levels are getting seriously low." Watkins sat next to him on the boulder. "That man's going to be the death of me." After he sat he looked at Philips directly. "Why are you over here all by yourself?"

"I'm not," Philips responded causing confusion to grow on Watkins's face. Philips chuckled, "You are here too."

Watkins smiled and shook his head.

"Damn, you need to work on your jokes because they are lacking. But seriously, you good?"

"Yeah," Philips paused for a moment, thought, then answered. "For the first time on this trip I think I see some light. You know?"

"Definitely. After all, look at this gift from God."

Philips looked away for a moment and Watkins caught on to the hint. That topic might have dampened the mood on what had been a relatively hopeful day. However, at the moment, it was more probable that his curiosity would do so. In spite of the immaculate discovery, he still had another thought creeping through his unsatisfied head.

Philips returned to eye contact.

"D.J. let me ask you something." His comment drew Watkins's full attention. "What do you know about Dr. Porter?"

"I mean I probably know just as much as anybody else in the crew." He was caught off guard by the question. "Why do you—"

"Dr. Porter, what do you want to know?" Watkins had been cut off by an oncoming person.

Philips and Watkins both looked ahead of them to find Thatcher walking in their direction. He walked with somewhat of a swagger due to the fact that he held information that they did not know.

He repeated, "What do you want to know?" He did not sit.

Philips was surprised by his seemingly random appearance. His question to Watkins had become like a male dog's urinary marking, attracting other's interests. Subsequently, he looked at the sharing frequency on his visor. The visor showed him that his frequency was turned off, so he attributed Thatcher's arrival to pure chance.

Philips—recognizing that he might lose his audience—asked, "Before this trip? Did you know him?"

"Are you telling me you had never heard of him prior to 'New Beginnings'?"

"Never," Philips said shaking his head at Watkins and back to Thatcher.

"Interesting. I guess he was just well-known in the science community then." Thatcher prepared himself to tell a story. "Dr. Nar Porter was one of the best scientists the world had ever seen. He was so good that he worked through the government directly." Thatcher had suddenly immersed both men into his story from the past. "He worked in nearly every field, but he had become noteworthy for his work in biology and genetics. For years, he had made ground breaking discoveries in the genetics of animals, plants, etc. Rumor has it that at one point he had even come close to a cure for cancer. The man changed generations of science and was intellectually miles ahead of most scientists in the world."

"What happened?" Philips asked.

"He still is truly, but so much changed the day his wife became sick."

"Sick?" Watkins's asked.

Thatcher disregarded Watkins's ignorance.

"His wife developed a disease during the early stages of pregnancy. It was a disease that no one could diagnose. No doctor knew what it was and no scientist had seen something to that extent. And truthfully, no one wanted to come in contact with it. He tried so desperately to cure it himself, but failed. Following the death of his wife and child, he disappeared for a few years. This voyage has been somewhat of his first appearance since." He stopped to conclude his own thoughts. "Honestly, I don't know what the colonel sees in the purpose of bringing him."

Philips was still unfulfilled. "That seems slightly inept, no offense. I just feel as though there is more to it."

"What can I say? The man is mysterious."

Thatcher was quick and short with his response. It was evident he did not enjoy Philips's response given that it had taken him effort to develop the synopsis.

"Well this Porter research is going to have to continue later," Watkins said pointing to the skyline behind Thatcher.

Thatcher turned to see what Watkins was pointing at and Philips simply looked beyond Thatcher's average frame. Along the scarcely dusk horizon was an aerial vehicle that was identical to their broken down Hawk. Its front lit the sky with a deep blue light that was blinding to stare at. It rumbled sound waves to its side, delivering Philip's ears with a rich, deep humming. As it got closer, the reduction of the sound waves declined to the point that they were fully prominent and vibrating a few yards from his head. The three watched the rest of the crew board the craft without questions, so they made their way over and did the same. They now began their flight back to the *New Sumeria*, leaving their new discoveries behind.

THE GENESIS OF BETRAYAL

Colonel Goodwin spaced out his timing just so that Mr. Dover was half way to his current destination. The ship was empty and quiet. The perfect time for him to complete his intended task. Yes, Avi was still the other overseer of the ship, thus making Goodwin's task somewhat secretive. Nonetheless, his plan had been concealed and he had no intention of deviating away from his caution.

He stood from his seat in the cockpit and formulated a lie for Avi.

"Avi keep a watchful eye on Dover and the crew." His disguises had become legendary. "I am going to check on Dr. Porter."

However, the last statement to Avi did ironically hold some truth. He would set his intended mental waypoint to the restricted area, but he needed to first make a pit stop. He figured that he had a few hours to do what he needed, but he had a slight hustle in his step because he did not want there to be any room for error. It was known that Avi would have her sights on Goodwin, but he assumed most of her attention would be directed towards the crew and less of him. This lead way, so to speak, was just enough to allow Goodwin to make the pit stop at his room.

He entered quickly and the door shut behind him, completely hiding him from Avi's watchful eyes. Goodwin was comfortable in some of the rooms aboard the ship because he had his ways to get around Avi's security. Ways he had not divulged to Dover or any other crew member. On his bedside table sat an unloaded handgun. He approached it from the side and swiped the gun from the surface of the table. A black grip along the handle of the firearm gave it a smooth yet adhesive grasp in his hand. Below the table was an automatic drawer, in which Goodwin pressed a button. The button caused it to open and uncover miscellaneous objects. Of the objects, Goodwin found what he desired, a rectangular cartridge. He shut the drawer and pushed the cartridge into the bottom of his handgun. His pit stop was complete, so he tucked the gun in his pants line and covered its top with his shirt. Though the outline of gun was sketched by the tight uniform, it would not be visible enough for Avi to see.

He reentered the hall, making himself susceptible to Avi's potential view. Even if Avi was monitoring Goodwin's every step, she would not find anything seemingly suspicious about him. In her animated mind, he was truly going to check on Dr. Porter. Goodwin had played his hand very well and found himself inside the restricted area. He pulled the gun from his pants and steadily held it in front of him. His arms were straight and the gun was held at a forty-five degree downward angle. From a partially turned position, the colonel rotated his step slowly until he was just before the two rooms. Both rooms were lit. One had a bright white appeal similar to the hall and the other held a glowing cherry red. He inspected the white room first by peeking his head and gun around to the front of the room. Looking through the glass door, it was empty. He turned sharply and focused on the red room. It was not lit very well. Shadows disbursed from every corner. Goodwin gripped his gun tightly as he slid passed the doors. He checked the front two corners by pointing his gun in their direction and did the same for the back. The room was empty as well.

A sigh of relief came from his mouth as he relaxed his arms and placed the gun at his side. Perspiration covered his forehead, for he could feel the intense radiating heat from the table in front of him. He loomed toward the table and saw the two spheres. They were peaceful and temporarily defenseless. Goodwin reached to grab one, but the red light flickered for a moment and made him withdraw his hand. When the light gathered itself and returned to a steady consistent radiance, he began to reach for it once more.

He reached slowly and became closer and closer to touching the eggs until his hand stopped completely. He felt an intensive pain drive its way into his shoulder causing him to drop the gun from his opposite hand. The pain was unbearable. It rushed through his veins and bloodstream restlessly. He let out an elongated groan of torment and agony as he fell to his knees. From behind him he noticed a figure, but he could not see it clearly. His vision had blurred and his strength had begun to deplete causing him to now fall to his hands as well. Attempting to use all his remaining vigor, he looked up towards the figure from a dog-like stance.

The figure spoke. "Now what would you be doing with my creation, Colonel Goodwin." Goodwin recognized the voice.

"I told you once before that you shouldn't touch them."

"Porter," Goodwin struggled to speak. "What, what did you…"

The pain had become too much for Goodwin to speak in complete sentences.

"Please, Colonel, save yourself from the anguish. I will simply tell you. This here," Porter said as he pulled a syringe out of Goodwin's back, "Is the virus in its liquidized form."

Porter held the syringe in between his fingers, shaking it gently as he spoke. The liquid inside of the syringe could have easily been mistaken for water due to its clear consistency.

He returned to his soliloquy.

"As you are coming to find out, the virus doesn't react well with humans." He sneered. "In fact, what makes this project so unique is that these organisms before us are unharmed by it. I have come to realize—in my studies—that the virus only harms creatures that are already fully developed organisms. However, here is the fascinating part, so you should pay attention." Goodwin coughed violently. "The virus can be used in the development of a growing species. Not only does it help the organism grow at a substantial rate, but because it is used in the creation, the virus in some ways becomes an essential ingredient in its genetics."

Porter flipped the syringe in his hand and caught it perfectly on the opposite side of the needle. He took it and placed it on the table, reaching over Goodwin's slowly dying body. He then spotted the handgun lying on the floor. Swiftly, his hand scooped it up and he began to examine it as he paced.

"So what was your plan? To shoot me and take my creation."

With an underhand release, he tossed the gun onto Goodwin. It hit him gently on the back and fell to the floor softly.

"It has become thematic with this virus, thriving off of death. As I look back on it now, Goodwin, I couldn't stand even the slightest thought of her death." He referenced his wife. "If it weren't for her disease, I would have never discovered this virus. I would have had the normal life I desired." He paused. "I loved her, Goodwin, and I wanted nothing more than to have a child with her. But disease, another imperfection of our world, plagued this chance. With my chances gone, I will try again but with this." He held his hand flat in the direction of the eggs. "The virus and my creation will be my new path."

He stopped pacing and thought hard on a concept. He had now been rambling.

"And with you, yes with you. It seems simple enough. You were hindering its development so you need to be taken care of."

Goodwin's pain was at a climatic high. He could not move his muscles and limbs. His vision had completely vanished leaving him with nothing but darkness. With one last final breath, the colonel pleaded.

"God, help me" he said as he fell completely to the ground.

Porter heard his plea and bent down in a squat. He leaned his lips over Goodwin's ear and whispered. "God?" he scoffed. "Save yourself the plea." He pulled away. "I am God."

Goodwin's heart stopped, and his body fell completely to the floor. His back faced the ceiling while his arms were resting at his side. His head was turned and his face had a lifeless stare.

Porter stood from his crouched position and gazed at the departed. He knew that if he had not killed Goodwin, then his plan would have been foiled. Goodwin's death was a sacrifice for Porter's ambition and intended perfection. All was due to change upon this action.

Subsequently, Porter's attention towards his justified murder was broken by a crackling sound. He looked up to the eggs to find that subject E was doing exactly what the sound expressed. A crack split the top of its egg causing pieces of shell to trickle to the table's surface. It was time, Porter thought. He studied the sphere intensely as it became mangled and disfigured. It had transformed from a perfectly smooth shape to a jumbled mess of white bits. However, he would soon find that this previous perfection would lead to a new perfection: the perfection of a being—a real entity.

Before him, a sand colored creature rose from the array of scattered egg. It was covered in a red, sticky essence that dripped from its body. The body of the creature was humanoid, mostly, consisting of a head and four limbs. Its oval head was relatively proportionate to the body, but its face was slightly different than that of a human's. There were two eyes and a mouth, but instead of a nose it had two small holes. As it completely exposed its bare body, Porter comprehended its whole. It was the size of a human baby, but it was much longer and skinnier. The body was not emaciated; it was leaner. Even for a new born species it was very much developed physically and despite its struggle to stand, it was able to stumble around the table. This task would have taken most species weeks, even months to do.

The creature's eyes searched the room until they met Porter's. Porter was uneasy, but calm at the same time as he reached his hand towards it. He stopped halfway in hopes of the creature meeting him at that point. There he held his hand for a moment. The creature somewhat recognized his gesture with a chirping hiss. Porter was not frightened by this as he held his ground. He assumed this was its attempt at communicating with him.

"Don't be afraid. I'm not going to hurt you." Porter realized that it would not understand him, but he simply spoke for the purpose of showing his gentle tone.

The statement was in fact reassuring for this new born creature as it lend its head towards his hand and brushed it against his fingers. The action was much like something a cat would do. Its skin was hard like protective layering almost; however, it was smooth to the touch.

"That's it."

Words could not begin to describe the emotions and thoughts that Porter generated. He had created life. In many ways it was in his image, but in many ways it was not. Yes, he had created it so that it was humanoid, but it seemed more efficient. He noticed there were no visible reproductive organs, and even though it was a female specimen, it had the same physical makeup as male. He had designed them to be identical so that neither sex would lack the physical benefits of the other. Both would share the same physical strength while carrying their necessary reproductive functions.

Porter pulled away having been pleased with the creature's reaction towards him. He back away and turned towards the door. It was apparent to him that if he wanted this beautiful creation to last, he would need to guide it in the beginning of its nourishment. The mess hall would have all he needed to help the creature fully develop. On that thought, he walked from the table and out of the room. As he walked out, he reached into his pocket and found his coin. With a flick of his thumb, the coin rotated into the air and back into his hand. His contentment was expressed through the action, for he had truly found his path.

MISSING IN ACTION

By the time the crew returned to the ship, Goodwin's plan had failed while Porter's had begun. The rescue Hawk landed in the bay and the crew met in the cockpit. There was no sign of Goodwin anywhere. They had been directed by him to meet in the cockpit prior to their exploration for a post-debriefing, but it was hard to do so without his presence. Dover called his name over the ship-wide speaker, addressing that the consultation was ready to begin. No answer, no sighting. Everyone was dispersed throughout the cockpit during this waiting game, unlike any previous meetings. This disorganization was a result of the absence of the colonel. In a way, the truth was that without Goodwin's orders there was no incentive for the crew to have organization.

Oddly enough, Philips still sat in the same seat he had always. His hands were pushed through his hair, resting atop his head. He saw nothing but the floor below him; however, it was the perfect image allowing him to think, bearing in mind its dullness. The floor was awaiting Philips's thoughts to fill it with life. It was his temporary drawing board so he mental drew out his ideas. First, he thought about the Hawk and why it had suddenly refused to work. He had never flown one before, but based off his experiences with similar vehicles he assumed that he would have felt some kind of warning sign earlier. Second was the random disappearance of the colonel. After all, this collaboration was

Goodwin's idea and for him not to show was obviously strange. And third, Philips had not yet developed a third, but was certainly aspiring to find it.

Surveying the area and crew that was amongst him had become something he was accustomed to doing. The mission had reached a point where its suspicion could not be avoided. His head lifted from the floor to its normal position. Before, most of the crew had simply casted away any suspicion, but now Philips could see the weariness in everyone's expressions. He observed a few people. Daniels, who had a soldier's instinct, held a tight gripped on his handgun. Granted, the oddity of the situation could feed hostility, but why would someone need a firearm for a debriefing. Daniels was suspect number one. Zuckerman quickly became suspect number two as Philips watched him sporadically move his head side-to-side and had single handedly given the phrase "head on a swivel" new meaning.

Philips played detective with every member in the cockpit, even Watkins. For each individual, he found at least one piece of evidence that made them suspect towards their current situation. There was too much sketchiness in the cockpit for him to make a general assumption. The work had deviated from finding information to more of a board game. He sighed and realized he needed to restart his approach. Then it hit him. In his analysis of the crew, he had neglected one person: someone who had ironically haunted his thoughts for the majority of the mission. Where was Dr. Nar Porter? He had not seen him ever since their arrival to the planet. Precipitously, the events had shifted away from coincidence to probable causation.

"Are we going to wait here all night?" Thatcher broke Philips's concentration.

"Do you suggest we look for the colonel?" Dover asked, moving away from his screens.

"No, I suggest we call it a day and do this tomorrow. For all we know, he is asleep."

"I doubt that." Philips interrupted. "It would be highly unprofessional."

"Well, these solutions are beneficial."

Philips had noticed that the crew's uneasiness to the weird series of events was beginning to express itself in their dialogue.

"Listen, I understand you all are probably apprehensive," Philips said, standing from his seat. "But the worst thing we can do right now is panic or even worse, turn on each other."

Daniels gripped his gun harshly at his side and spoke. "I'd like to know how all of the sudden you have placed yourself in charge. We are not on Earth so I don't think military rankings apply."

"This here is a prime example of what I am talking about," Philips said without looking at Daniels. "Corporal if you could, please disarm your firearms."

Daniels heard Philips clearly, yet continued to stare. As he waited for Philips to counter his ranking statement, he slowly offered at Philips's request. His hand met the weapon and with a motion the cartridge was removed.

"You are right, Corporal, but seeing that Colonel Goodwin had put me in charge during his absence I do feel as though I should have some say in what goes on. Of course, if that's okay with everyone else."

Everyone agreed with a head nod, accept for Daniels. Dover had also agreed that it was best to have a qualified officer heading the decisions of the ship, provided that he had done so the entire mission thus far. It was not Philips intension to become supreme leader of this planet, let alone the ship. He simply just wanted to ensure the safety and sanity of the crew. Also, by now he understood that Daniels acted the way he had during the mission because he wanted a chance to lead. Most-likely, Philips attributed, Daniels wanted to prove himself after Avi had scolded him during their first debriefing.

"Daniels?" he said attempting to draw a head nod.

Daniels paused for a moment and responded Philips the desired gesture.

"All right," Daniels said softly. "What's the plan?"

"I think the best thing to do is to call it a day. We will put together a ship-wide search tomorrow. I think this will allow everyone to relax and take a step back."

The plan was finalized.

FINDING MORE THAN WHAT THEY BARGAINED FOR

Upon the rising of Exodus's sun, the cockpit was once again in their place of meeting. Still there was no sign of Colonel Goodwin or Dr. Porter so Philips gave his orders. He designated an area of the ship for the crew members keeping them in the same groups they had during their planetary exploration. However, this time Philips remained back with Dover in the cockpit so that he could monitor and analyze.

Watkins and Rodriguez were assigned to the residence area of the ship. They walked slowly with each other, side by side. The hallways showed no sign of any life other than themselves. Surprisingly, there was a light atmosphere as they walked. Each step between them made it seem as though they were on a gradual stroll through the ship.

"It's funny how we are on a new planet, but we're instead exploring the ship," Rodriguez said.

"I guess that's what we get when we don't even fully understand our own kind," Watkins returned.

"How do you mean?" she asked as Watkins opened the doors to the rooms and checked inside.

Watkins held a handgun just to be safe. "Well, it seems hard to analyze other life when we don't have a full grasp of ourselves." They looked through the rooms; they were clear.

"Agreed, but don't you think that we can solve a lot of humanities problems through discovery?"

"To some extent." Watkins was wise for his Earthly occupation. "I just think that people try to force ideas to others through their own experiences. They don't realize that not everybody is the same."

"Deep Watkins," Rodriguez smiled. "Is this a religious discussion?"

"I wouldn't say religion so much."

"All right then, what?"

"Whatever you want. Whatever you want to call it. Your path can be whatever you choose. For example, you are a scientist. You choose to explain things through scientific proof. That is your path. People don't realize that you cannot force someone to follow in the same footsteps. If that were the case, then people would follow blindly."

"But what if my 'path' leads me to the proof that your 'path' is wrong."

"And this is where the world can be wrong itself. People spend more time trying to disprove each other than actually questioning what they themselves believe in." Watkins stopped searching for a moment and stared at Rodriguez. "People's paths can only take them so far. At some point you have to put your faith into something. Just remember, faith is confidence in what we hope for and assurance about what we do not see."

"Yeah, I will keep that mind, Watkins," she said sarcastically.

Watkins was lighthearted towards her tone.

"You joke, but once people understand that our paths don't need to be the same, then we truly understand our own kind."

Watkins discussion ended abruptly as he found himself unable to open one of the rooms. He looked to the wall beside the door. "Colonel J. Goodwin" it read. Watkins reached towards his head and pressed a device that sat on his ear. This device had been handed to each of the searching members so that they could be in direct contact with Dover and Philips. It was more efficient than forcing Avi to circulate through the ship every time someone reported evidence.

"We have something interesting here," he said into the single-pieced headset.

"What's that?" Dover asked from the cockpits central communication.

"Goodwin's room is locked." Watkins knocked on the door. "Colonel, are you in there?"

There was no answer.

"Have Avi unlock it," Philips said to Dover.

Avi searched through the ship's data base and found the task impossible for her to do. She made herself visible on the screens before Dover and Philips.

"Mr. Dover it seems I cannot open the door." Avi expressed no tone, but her choice of words yielded concern.

Dover moved closer to the screen and began to play with the different images. He dialed and typed on the screen, but could not find anything he hoped for.

"Odd. It appears that something is hindering Avi's ability to open some of rooms aboard." He said it for the group to hear. "Avi, access the security tapes for—." He searched for the areas on the ship that Avi had been prevented from. "Goodwin's residence and the restricted area."

Philips trembled at the mention of the restricted area. It was almost so obvious that they had overlooked it. The typical person would have agreed that the warning signs were suspicious. However, Goodwin had been so reassuring that everyone aboard seemed to not dwell on them.

"I cannot access these either," Avi proclaimed.

Dover crunched a few numbers and formulas into the screen. He pondered for a moment until there it was. The truth was in plain sight.

"Lieutenant, you were right," Dover disclosed.

"Right about what?" Philips asked.

"The virus," Dover turned to Philips exposing his anxiety. "Goodwin had been using the computer virus to hide things from Avi and the rest of us. He sabotaged her right underneath our noses. The restricted area, his residence, the nuclear room, hell even communications with Earth—all infected."

"Don't you see?" Philips asked. "He made it so obvious that we simply ignored it all. No one would think that he would make something such as this so evident."

"But why?"

"This mission isn't for exploration. It is for something else. Can you reboot whatever Goodwin corrupted?"

"Yes, but with this virus it would take me awhile to fix this."

"How long are we talking?"

"There's no telling really." Dover sighed.

"Okay, I want you to fix this while I attempt to figure this out." Philips redirected his speech to the screens. "Sergeant Watkins and Corporal Daniels, meet me in weaponry. The rest of the crew, return back to the cockpit immediately."

Dover walked away from the screens and stopped in his path.

"What are going to do?" He asked as he tossed a headset to Philips.

The two put in their headsets simultaneously.

"I need to go to the restricted area. I think there is someone who knows what's going on."

WHAT DOESN'T KILL THEM
MAKES THEM STRONGER

Daniels, Thatcher, and Zuckerman had been standing in a different area of the ship than Watkins and Rodriguez. The announcement from Philips had echoed through their headsets and into their eardrums. Thatcher and Zuckerman took the message as an order, while Daniels took it as more of a suggestion. As the two began to walk towards the cockpit, they noticed that Daniels matriculated in the opposite direction. They both stopped and turned back to him once they noticed.

"Daniels, the weapons room is this way." Thatcher spoke with his thumb pointed in their intend direction.

"Yeah, I know." Daniels turned to face them. "I'll meet with Philips and Watkins in a second. I just want to check something out."

"Okay, suit yourself." The two disappeared in the opposite direction.

Something had caught the eye of Daniels as he made his way around the corner of the hall. It was like a beam of light from an alien space craft pulling him in. However, it was nothing of extravagance. It was simply an open door, figuratively and literally. Daniels approached it with his handgun angled out in front of him. A voice interrupted his motion, temporarily causing him to stop.

"Come in, Daniels. Where are you?" Philips was waiting on him with Watkins in the weapons room.

His finger met the headset and ended the voice. He did not want to be distracted away from what was ahead of him. He returned back to his pursuit. As he passed through the wide-open door way, he read the sign on the wall, Restricted Zone. It was a quick glance at the words, but honestly it did not hold much meaning for him. He was more attracted to the open door.

Down the area's hallway interior, Daniels saw a strobe light flashing from the right side. Just as the open door had drawn him, so did this light. The closer he got to the light, the more his face glowed with a cherry red. Ignoring the room to the left, he entered the red room. He nearly dropped his gun at the sighting, but was able to instead hang on. At first, he did not make the connection of who it was, but once he was standing over the body he knew. He knelt to the floor and slowly rolled the body over to its backside. Goodwin's pale face was nonetheless startling, but his ogling, dead eyes were frightening. Daniels, with a smooth stroke of his hand, closed Goodwin's eyes. There was relief from the eeriness of the dead.

He rose from his squatted stance. His grief was ephemeral, if there was any, as he found himself drawn to another attention. The table in front of him was a mess. He started with the left side of it and shifted his eyes to the right, just as he would if he was reading. On the table's left side was something comparable: the same dishes that they had used to eat from in the mess hall. With his index finger, he wiped the inside of the dish and held the residue close to his nose. The smell was similar. From an assumption, he placed his finger in his mouth and tasted it. The taste was similar. He questioned why the food dishes were in this room and not in the in their rightful place. However, he did not dwell.

Despite seeing Goodwin's dead body, he had not expressed any signs of significant emotion to that point. Death had been something he had witnessed numerously before. These sightings were merely suspicious. However, as he continued to read the table's top, fear began to sneak its way into Daniels. Next to the dishes were two soft shelled containers that sat side by side. Their tops had been mangled and completely torn to pieces while the insides were completely empty. Not knowing what the objects were struck him with this fear, yet he picked up a piece of one of the shells. The piece had lain by the side of the eggs and was large enough to inspect. With his fingers rubbing together smoothly, he felt the texture until the shell cracked and fell to pieces.

He was now afraid but tried to cover his emotions with a soldier's attitude. All of his fear was transferred to aggression as he gripped his handgun tighter and tighter. The blood in his hand faded quickly, leaving his fingers pale. A chill was sent through his spine and the hair on his neck rose. However, it was not the eggs that conjured his fear now, but something else—something behind him. He could feel the presence of something. He could feel its hot air breathing down his backside. Like a secret, the puffing air invited him to turn. It begged his curiosity. His fear could not be tamed; his emotions were no longer soldiered away. He had to turn to see what was toying with his mind. So he did.

Daniels breathed heavily as he turned. His heart raced to its own inconsistent pace. But, what he saw did not brush his fear away, it magnified it. There were no tricks being played throughout his mind. What he felt and sensed was real. The entity standing before him was a foot or so taller than himself and seemed to bounce slowly as it breathed. It stood in a powerful, staggered stance with its arms spread at its side. Its stance bestowed peacefulness and physical dominance, allowing itself to act on either. Both Daniels and the creature stood face to face, but there was an imminent amount of insecurity between them.

Sweat dipped from Daniels forehead as his heart exploded through his chest with each pump. He held the steady white knuckled grip upon his gun. In somewhat of an effort to gauge Daniels, the creature hissed. Daniels took this communicative chirp as a threat and drew his weapon sharply: one shot followed by two and then two by three until the clip was completely emptied. The creature had been pushed back by the shots, but the bullets did not seem to carry the same fatal effect against them as it did for humans. It noticeably bled, but the bullets only made it angrier and more hostile. With its growing rage, it smacked Daniels with one clean swipe of its arm. Daniels flew against the wall violently, smashing his skull. The creature hissed one last time as blood rushed from Daniels head. The red liquid spread its way across the floor and the creature fled the scene.

THE MOST DANGEROUS EMOTION

A few hours passed and Philips paced the area near the guns and ammo rack. He had become extremely impatient during their wait for Daniels. Watkins leaned his back against the wall next to the rack and crossed his arms.

"You think he heard the order," Watkins asked as he watched Philips pace.

"Yes, I just think he ignored it." Philips returned.

Philips pushed his headset with one final hope.

"Come in, Daniels."

Philips stopped walking and waited for a response. Neither man heard a sound from either of their headsets.

"Even if he had ignored the order, it wouldn't have taken him this entire time to search his assigned area," Watkins explained.

"So you think something happened to him?"

"There's always the possibility."

Philips paused with a glance at the ground. He pondered the thought and returned his finger to his headset.

"Avi?" Philips looked up now.

"Lieutenant Philips," Avi answered.

"Who is in the cockpit right now?"

"All of the scientists, just as you ordered. Is there something you need?"

"No, just have them stay there and report to me if anyone leaves."

"Yes, Lieutenant."

Philips ended the connection with Avi and redirected it to another frequency.

"Dover."

"Yes, Lieutenant." Dover's voice entered his ear.

"How's Avi's virus?"

"It might be a while longer. I've never had to disable and clear one of my viruses."

Dover chuckled on the other line.

"All right, keep working with it. Watkins and I are going to explore the ship." He sighed. "Daniels never returned."

With those last words, Philips grabbed a rifle and loaded it. Watkins did the same and they exited the ship's weapons room. The halls were white as always, but they seemed darker in their atmosphere. Weird events had taken place in the last day or so and the crew, especially Philips, had a steadily growing fear. They took each step carefully with their eyes bouncing around every wall and corner.

Philips had a destination in mind and led Watkins to that spot. So much mystery had come from the restricted area and so he thought it appropriate to go there. In his mind, he found that the places that had most questions and mystery were typically the places where one would find the most answers—an ironic belief at that but somewhat holds truth.

They reached the restricted area, acting as those who had done so before them. They too were drawn towards the red light and it seemed as though the third reassurance of this action was destine to repeat the same result. However, the third time was a charm, in the sense that Philips and Watkins carried fully lethal rifles. Also, there was no immediate threat at the moment. They scanned the red room first and found the bodies of the men who had gone missing. However, Philips had not found what he was in search of.

"My God!" Watkins exclaimed.

Watkins knelt to Daniels's body. The heels of his feet settled in pools of dark red that stretched relatively close to the door's entrance. He took two fingers and placed them on the body's neck, just below the jaw. He already knew the result of the action; however, he felt more civilized in at least attempting. Philips watched Watkins for a moment then walked and stood over the colonel's body.

Philips studied Goodwin's body closely.

"He looks like he has been dead a while."

"Murder?" Watkins asked. "Only logical explanation."

"I wouldn't be too sure of that."

Philips had been referencing his uncertainty to the eggs that resided on the table. He walked up to them and kind of leaned toward them to see what they were. He did not want to get too close for his lack of full knowledge.

"What do you make of that?" Watkins asked.

"I don't know. I have never seen anything like this." He paused and changed his thought. "I have to make sure Dover is safe." He activated his communications. "Dover?"

Dover heard and responded. "I am almost there, Lieutenant. I am just running a program. It is loading at the moment."

"Can the program run on its own?"

"Yes, it would just take longer without me."

"Forget the program and the virus. I need you to get to safety. Goodwin and Daniels are dead. Someone or something is killing the crew. We need to find a safe area and stick together."

"What? What do you mean?"

"That's exactly what I mean. People are dying."

"Okay, I will go to the cockpit with the others."

"Perfect. We will meet you there shortly."

Philips knew that he needed to come and find what he was in search of. So he tucked his rifle to his shoulder and crept his way out of the red room. He entered the hall and stopped. Watkins did the same. He eyed the room across the way and noticed that the light had been turned off completely. The darkness filled him with a peculiar feeling that he had never sensed before. There was fear building, but for some reason the fear seemed to give him an obligation. He felt that he must explore the dark room to find what it concealed in order to protect the crew from any future dangers. The doors were opened making it easy for Philips to sneak the barrel of his rifle through the entrance. He put his hand to the wall and felt it softy, searching for a switch of some kind. The brushing of the wall lasted a while until the tips of his fingers met an object that stuck out. He pushed it and the lit the dark.

He gathered his rifle quickly to his shoulder and Watkins matched him to his side. They both pointed their rifles at the creature that stood across the room from them. Without hesitation, the creature leaped to the wall to their right and continuously bounded from all angles of the room. It had gone from standing on two legs to crawling around the rooms surface's on all fours. The soldiers fired irregularly, with the hope of shooting the creature. However, it was nearly impossible. Their bullets hit the walls rather than the flesh of the being. Finally, it made itself presentable by attacking Watkins. Watkins fell hard to the ground creating a sound like a bowling ball dropping on a tile surface. With the creature on top of him, Watkins could hardly breathe from its weight. It swiped at his torso like a bear mauling a human. The bullets at first did not affect it very much, but after a series of the metal puncturing the same spot repeatedly, the creature slowed. The rifle vibrated harshly against the ligaments in Philips's shoulder, but he held strong. He resisted his stoppage until the gruesome attack ended and the creature fell lifelessly.

"Christian..." Watkins could barely speak. The air had been taken from his lungs.

Philips rushed over to Watkins after he had seen that the creature's immaculate size was crushing Watkins. He rolled it off of him and to the empty flat floor that was next to them. He looked at the creature, identifying what it was, but he could not make a clear connection. It looked human, but it was also far from it. It was bare and its features were human-like. Nonetheless, it was much longer and had better muscular tone and development. He found his kill shot, or rather kill shots, and placed his hand on the wound. The skin was hard, and the blood that secreted from its inside was red and dark. He wiped the red consistency on his uniform, smearing a stain down his side. He then moved his focus to his friend. Watkins coughed a little and scattered red liquid dispersed from his mouth.

"We have to get you out of here," Philips exclaimed.

Philips tried to give him hope, but the truth was that Watkins had suffered substantial injuries from this thing. His face and neck were completely bruised and his chest and stomach had deep, wet tints that grew as they spoke.

"What is this place?" Watkins tried to pull himself up to see what was around them.

Noticing his strain, Philips gently pushed Watkins back to his laying position. Then he did what Watkins could not and examined the room for him. Surrounding them were roughly twenty eggs that were scattered throughout the room. Each one had been cracked open and had pieces of adjacent shell. The emotion of the moment was almost unbearable for Philips. Not only was he dealing with his dying friend, but also the potential of more of these creatures. He did not have a definitive solution to any of these erratic occurrences and at this point; he had to do things based on what he thought was the best. There was no guaranteed happy ending available. Everything from now on was survival.

"Come on." Philips picked up Watkins and slung Watkins's arm over his shoulder. Watkins's legs were limp causing Philips to partially drag his friend.

"Dover, come in Dover." Philips directed to his headset.

"Yes, Lieutenant." Dover was alert as a result of Philips concerned tone.

"Watkins is hurt badly."

"From what?"

"We don't know what it was, some kind of creature. Whatever it was it was hostel and tried to kill us."

"How do you know this?"

"Because we saw it!"

Watkins's weight was heavy on Philips shoulder, but his will conquered the physical presence. He carried him all the way to the cockpit. Once he was in the cockpit he hollered for help and the others came to his side. Philips placed Watkins on the first flat surface he could find. After dropping him on a table near the monitors, he backed away and found a seat. There he sat in shock, watching the crew grab whatever supplies they could to help heal Watkins. He knew it was only a matter of time before Watkins would pass, for he had seen internal injuries such as his before and knew that no man would survive them without a proper doctor. In essence, they needed someone with a medical expertise and not a scientist.

They were falling victim to this mission one at a time. His shock continued as he stared off into space. The other members in the cockpit were a blur. He had not found what he was looking for in the restricted area. Everyone was slightly blind to it; however, to Philips, it was clear. *Why would a man disappear prior to a series of unfortunate events? Responsibility was strongly correlated to his flee,* Philips thought. *Who is this man, this Doctor Narayan Porter?* The room began to spin and his eyes began to close. The shock had gotten the best of him.

MEANINGS

Philips awoke to the dripping of water down his face. He reached his hand to his head and wiped the water from his nose. Its source was a wet towel that someone must have placed upon his forehead when he slipped away. He peeled the towel from his head and it dribbled a few droplets onto the floor as he stood. Looking around, he saw that the crew was asleep, either lying against the wall or in a seat. Everyone was asleep except for Mr. Dover, who stood over Sergeant Watkins. Philips made his way over to the two and empathetically examined his friend. His uniform shirt had been removed, exposing his bare torso. On his torso were deep lacerations and bruises that dispersed their way from his shoulders to his navel. Dover spoke, but Philips continued to inspect Watkins's injuries.

"We have him pretty drugged up right now," Dover said. "The truth is… his internal bleeding is too much for us to handle. Without a medical doctor, he is most-likely going to die. It's only a matter of time really."

Philips looked at Watkins's eyes. They were completely yet softly shut. The drugs had allowed him to peacefully fade into a place of comfort and relaxation. Philips knew the realization Dover had told him before he had actually said anything. In a positive sense, he thought, this ability was a benefit that military combat had granted him. He had learned to determine when a wound was too fatal for a recovery—a disparaging approach however it helped give a soldier shorter and less vigorous periods of grief.

Dover walked away from the table and to his screens. He either recognized that Philips wanted his time with Watkins or he wanted to check on the progress of his program. Possibly, it was both. Philips leaned his elbows against the chest-high table. His hands were held together and his head rested on them. He let out an elongated breath and eased himself.

"Is this a prayer I see?" Watkins voice was soft and barely noticeable.

Philips pulled his forehead from his hands and turned his head to the side so that he faced him. He was awake from his deep sleep, but was hardly aware. Philips smiled as he looked at his friend.

"How are you feeling?" Philips asked.

"Well...considering I'm on drugs...I don't feel much," he faintly replied.

"You look good, like you are going to pull through." Philips reassured.

"Don't do that Christian...We both know." Watkins smiled and slowly shook his head.

"I'm sorry, D.J."

"Don't be...I chose to come here. And even though...I didn't know what it held for me...I don't doubt that I served my purpose...in some way."

"So you think your purpose for this mission was to die." Philips's whispered, but his voice grew erratic.

"That's one way to say it...One horrible and demeaning way...I would say that my purpose was to find you...and show you how to find the goodness in the world."

Philips looked down, sighed, and back up to Watkins. "And where's the goodness in death?" Philips had a stern look upon his face. "It only shows the evils in the world, or universe for that matter." Philips corrected himself, realizing that they were far from Earth.

"No, Christian…You're looking at it all wrong…Evil is necessary…Without the bad, we wouldn't know what's good… And without the good…we wouldn't know what's bad…It might be hard to believe…but they thrive off each other."

"I could live without evil in the world, D.J. You don't need evil."

Watkins closed his eyes for a moment and reopened them. "But, after a while…you would lose the concept of what's truly good…Evil is there for the purpose of reminding us… but as humans we try to defeat it…We fight so that we can defend the good…We need it so we can discover what we fight for…what we believe in."

His voice grew weaker and he tried his best to force his eyes to stay open. Philips sensed that his death was nearing. However, Watkins would not die without delivering his final words of wisdom. Something that he was destined to do. With his final few breaths, he gathered and formed them into his speech.

"Sometimes we have this evil so…we can see the goodness in the world." He was fading quickly. "You will reach a time when you see the good…This time will come and you…you will defend it…and defend what you believe."

Watkins's eyes were blinking. His chest moved up and down for a moment. It was slow. Instantly it grew heavy and violently raised and lowered. It was brief and eventually his chest stopped moving. It was quiet in the cockpit. There was no pain or regret in the atmosphere around Watkins's dead body, only peace. He had succeeded in his purpose and had planted a seed. Though Philips had not known it just yet, Watkins's words would carry more meaning than he had expected. It was only a matter of time that this seed would blossom into something greater.

Philips placed his hand on Watkins's chest and flattened his palm. There was no heart beat and no air passing through his lungs. He closed his hand into a fist, enclosing on Watkins's dog tags. With a quick yank, he pulled the dog tags clean from his neck and pocketed them. However, he had not left Watkins's bare. He left his faith and belief with his body to rest. Upon his chest remained Watkins's crucifix, connected to a chain that wrapped around his neck. For a moment, he envied Watkins. He knew that in whatever way Watkins had died, he would never die alone.

From his leaning position, he moved away from the table and walked over to Mr. Dover. He stood there for a moment before Dover actually noticed that Philips was standing next to him. Turning away from his screens, he found Philips staring at him. From the plain look on his face, Dover sensed Philips's emotionless and almost confused state.

"He's gone," Philips said.

"I'm truly sorry." I know he was your friend and the truth was that we all liked him."

"Yeah."

Philips reached to a nearby table and grabbed an idol handgun. He felt its weight to ensure that it was load and pulled the cartridge from the firearm to be assured. The gun was loaded. He tucked it into the waistline of his back side, just above his rear. Then he returned to Dover.

"What exactly happened, Lieutenant?"

Dover had told the others about Philips encounter with a creature, but no one knew the details.

"There is something aboard."

"What do you mean something?"

"When we went to the restricted room, we found Goodwin and Daniels both dead. Goodwin's death was clean, but Daniels, Daniels's head was smashed violently by something. We didn't think much of it, just the possibility of murder or something, but then we found eggs. These eggs were cracked open and then we found more in another room. There must have been dozens." Philips breathed intensely at the thought. "Then we saw it, some creature. It was humanoid, but it was larger and much more physically developed. It didn't even think twice about attacking us."

"Do you think these things are indigenous to the planet?"

"No." Philips shook his head. "I think somehow all this, the planet, the computer virus, these creature, they are all connected…" He looked away. "…We need answers."

"But…how?"

"When we went to the restricted room originally, I was looking for someone."

"Who?"

"Dr. Porter." Philips paused at the name. "There's something about this man. He hides himself away. He has made himself invisible."

"Will you go search for him?"

"I suppose." Philips changed his topic. "Are communications online yet?"

"They are close, but I can't activate it from here. I have to go back to the nuclear room."

"Okay." Philips devised a plan. "I will find Porter and interrogate him, while you activate communications." Philips started walking away and stopped. "Oh and Dover, take a weapon this time, you might need it."

Their jobs were set: Dover would reset communications while Philips would look for Porter. Dover's task seemed slightly easier considering he knew exactly where to go. He walked out of the cockpit with Philips, but once the two had separated, his journey seemed endless. Philips's story of creatures had amplified Dover's heart rate. He had not given it much thought when they discussed it, but somehow his current isolation brought suspense out of the story. As he walked down the silent corridors, he could sense every motion and sound. Every step he took sounded like his boots had been hooked up to a subwoofer, blasting its bass against the white walls. His body temperature rose a few degrees giving him the appearance of a slowly roasted piece of pork.

Wiping the sweat from his brow was almost pointless seeing that each time he did his forehead would simply grease itself again.

On the other hand, Philips was calm in demeanor. He had seen the creature which had given him an advantage in some sense. On his back, he had strapped a rifle and in his hand, he held a handgun. His steps were not nearly as loud as Dover's and his forehead stayed relatively dry. The fear had passed him now; however, he was somewhat angry—angry at Watkins's death as well as the creature, but most of all angry at its potential source; it fueled him as he walked intensely through the corridors of his destination, despite its lack of specificity and definitiveness.

Dover began to quiver making it hard to hold his gun in his slick hand. He adjusted his grip a few times, but each time the gun would slide down his hand and though his fingers. Growing frustrated with this continuous process, he tucked the weapon between his neck and chin and wiped his hands down his uniform. He then relocated the firearm back to his hand and continued to walk.

Philips expressed a passion and had reached the mess hall in no time. He slid through its door way, gun held at eye level. He scanned each corner, but there was no sign of present life. On the contrary, he saw the effects of life. The refrigerator, which held months' worth of food for the crew, had its door ripped off and its insides picked clean. Philips noticed the remnants of a few dishes and scraps, but the refrigerator was for the most part unable to provide any future meals. He walked over to the broken dishes and stepped through them in order to examine it further. With each step, there was a crackling from the sole of his boots. To the side, he picked up the refrigerator's door and inspected what was underneath it. There was nothing but further dishes and smeared grey mush. He set the door down and turned back. Someone, or something rather, had scavenged through their only food supply. This expedition was now introducing new challenges and furthering itself into this game of survival.

Making his way back to the hall, he reached for his headset to tell Dover the news of their food supply but abruptly stopped. He quickly dropped to the floor and forced his back to a table. He could hear something from the hall; however, he could not decipher its sound. He listened closely and heard a series of weird sounds weaving together in sequences. One sound was met by another of a different tone. He slowed his breathing down so that he could identify them fully. The sounds became closer and closer until he could tell that they were directly outside the doorway. There was snapping and popping like one would make with their tongue. But these tongued noises were rhythmic and held some purpose. The tones flew through the air and swam inside his eardrums. As he listened, he realized that they were doing much more than making a racket. They were communicating and that this was their language. In a way, the language was surprisingly sophisticated in its nature and, for a brief moment, Philips became lost in how civilized it was.

They closed the distance between them and Philips's hiding spot, causing him to snap from his daze. The only thing separating him from the creatures was an aluminum based table. He turned and looked underneath the table and saw a pair of bare, flesh-toned legs. The legs bent paradoxically with their awkward yet athletic stance. The creature was nearly on top of the table and Philips thought his safety had been undoubtedly compromised. It stopped communicating with the other and dug its feet deeply into the floor. With a great puff of air, the creature seemingly scoffed at the situation and turned away. Philips's hiding spot must have been angled perfectly, for the creature failed to see even the top of his head. Celebrating his partial victory of hide-and-seek, he watched the legs exit the door and make their way down the hall.

A sigh of relief left Philips's lungs as picked himself up slowly. He rested one arm on the table and the other held his gun high. He surveyed his surroundings and designated that the room was indeed clear. Just to ensure his future safety, he hit the wall next to the doorway with his back and peered out into the hall. The corridor was empty and the creatures were gone.

A snail's pace would have been an understatement for Dover's current walking speed. He was not terribly far from the nuclear room, but his mounting fear gave him the feeling that he was miles away. He could see the end of the hall. It was a perpendicular hallway, two directions to turn. But, as he stared at the back wall more and more, it seemed to gradually pull itself away from him. He shook head in order to readjust his perception and the wall returned to its original position. He stopped once more to rationalize his thinking. He was almost there, he reassured himself. However, fate would show that his destination was not destined to be met.

From the ceiling, a creature dropped down behind him. Dover heard the feet of the creature hit the ground hard causing him to turn, gun pointed. Before Dover could discharge his weapon he was thrown to the floor. The sound of bones rang through the ship like wood to tile contact. His headset scattered across the floor, but he still held on to his handgun. Spotting the earpiece from the corner of eye, he straightened his hand and gripped what he could of the sweat slickened floor. Each pull was not successful as he slipped to the floor numerously. He fired his weapon, hoping to gain an advantage. The bullets were almost pointless as so was his effort. He scrambled hard, but could not seem to gain any ground. He turned his focus completely to the headset, with his entire upper body reaching and grabbing for some form of leverage. However, despite all of his strength, the creature's strength was simply overpowering.

Philips found himself back in the hallway system of the ship. He had forgotten about his attempt to contact Dover, for the spotting had unsurprisingly distracted him. The searching grind continued as Philips was entering the residence area of the ship. He had not thought to look in Dr. Porter's room in order to find him. He thought it would be almost too easy. However, he had already once been fooled by this assumption. Under that thought, Philips stood in front of Porter's room. At this moment, he expected anything. The door was unexpectedly unlocked so he opened it. It parted quickly, but his aim was quicker and led the way. The room was just as empty as the refectory. Ignoring its apparent vacancy, Philips continued to walk into the room. It was dull, no clothes, no toiletries. The walls, bed, and tables were completely bare except for one object. Philips looked closely at this flat object that resided on a circular table. He looked hard and realized that the object was flat and black. He slowly approached it and placed himself over top. Once he had a clear view, he discovered it was a folder. Slowly and carefully his hand opened the folder and inspected its interior.

In its inside there were pictures and descriptions of each of the crew members. The order of personal appeared to be alphabetical by last name, with the first name showing *Corporal Michael Daniels*. Below his name he read his job description and background, the routine information. He continued to read down the page until he became stuck on a part that read *Status*. He slowly passed his eyes over the word and the colon that separated it from another. As he glanced at the following word, a great deal of confusion mounted him.

"Expendable." he read aloud to himself.

Philips flipped to the page that followed. The second name that appeared before him was *Stephen Dover*. He skimmed through the description and found the desired section of his status, and again, to its right, it read: *Expendable*. Growing anxious, he began to rapidly flip through the pages with purpose. After he read the names, he would look for the status. With each turn of the page, he found the same word pasted in red ink. This process continued until he sharply stopped his aggressive flipping. He was fixed on a new picture and name that presented itself on the laminated paper. Scanning over the letters at the top of the page, he examined the deftly formed letters of his name. He closed his eyes and took a deep breath, preparing himself for the future the document portrayed. As he reopened his eyes, his stomach felt like he had just experienced the gravitation effects of a free fall. There it was once again. The dreaded words were written so candidly next to his "Status."

He backed away from the folder quickly, bumping his backside into Porter's bed. He placed his open hand upon his head and stared and continued to stare. It was clearly alarming, but he did not fully understand what it meant. A gust of curiosity hit him with force, and he removed his hand from his head, finding the folder once more. He opened it and scanned the names. The folder accounted for seven of the nine humans. Cycling through the pages repetitively, it was apparent. There was no Colonel Goodwin or Dr. Porter. With one last close, he tucked the folder into his armpit and exited the room. Deductive reasoning showed him that he now needed to find him.

Returning to his search, he had grown irritated with the fact that he could not find Dr. Porter. The ship was large, but he had checked the three main areas that he was most-likely to be in. He now realized that the failure to find Porter could result in his expendability. He checked one of the rooms at a time, even checking his own, not leaving anything to chance. But there was no sign of Porter. With a few rooms left to check, he found himself standing before the colonel's room. Remembering that the room had been locked when Watkins attempted to open it, he reached his hand towards the door and pushed a button. He held his handgun in front of his head and looked down the barrel as the door opened.

To his surprise, not only did the door open, but there was a dark figure standing across the room from him, overlooking Goodwin's circular table. He had heard Philips open the door, but he did not move. He kept his eyes fixed on something in his hand. Philips looked to his torso and saw that he had been holding a picture of some sort. It glistened in the light, but it was blurry due to the distance that separated them.

Without looking at Philips, Porter spoke in his direction.

"Lieutenant Philips." He seemed uninterested in Philips's presence.

Philips pointed the gun at him and held his sight tightly. "This room was locked before. How did you get in here?"

"I have my ways."

Porter found a seat next to the table and rested himself in it. Once he was comfortable, he slid the piece of paper into his pocket. He now changed his interest to Philips, eyeing the handgun he possessed.

"We both know that wasn't one of the questions that have been picking your mind apart."

He crossed his arms and legs as Philips slowly migrated over to the table. Philips carefully aligned himself so that he was directly in front of Porter.

"What is going on, Porter?" Philips increased the intensity in his tone as he dropped the folder on the table. "I want the truth!"

Porter dismissed his crossed arms briefly as he reached towards the table. Philips watched consciously down the handgun's smoothly finished exterior. Porter's hand found the folder and with a gentle push, he slid it back to Philips.

"What is this?" Philips asked, recognizing that Porter had full knowledge of its meaning.

"You tell me?" Porter returned to his crossed position.

"I am not playing these goddamn games anymore Porter." Philips was angry with Porter's ability to avoid certain matters. "I want answers."

Porter chuckled at Philips, but Philips stayed completely serious with his handgun held steady.

"I am surprised that you haven't yet figured it out. All of your suspicion seems wasted at this point doesn't it?"

"I want answers Porter!"The gun became closer to Porter's head.

He could see the anger in Philips eyes; however, he knew that Philips was not going to discharge his weapon. He could read him so thoroughly that he could tell Philips did not have the ability to kill someone in cold blood. Rather, Porter, on the contrary, wanted to disclose this information. To him, it was not Goodwin's plan that mattered but his own.

"Your answers then." Porter prepared himself with a deep breath of his own. "This was no mission of discovery. Granted, *New Sumeria* explored this planet, but the government could have sent a robot to do that. The government had its sights on something else. They wanted a biological weapon. Something that could be sent to areas of conflict and war and simply wipe out the enemy—an idea that would dissolve the standard soldier and save countless numbers of lives."

"These creatures," Philips said softly under his breath.

"Yes, these creatures." Porter heard him. "My creation."

Philips was drawn towards Porter's word choice and recognized its significance. However, Porter did not allow for Philips to comment as he continued to speak.

"See Goodwin was placed in charge of this mission and told to put together a crew. The idea was for Goodwin to make this mission seem like an expedition—scientist, military, everything necessary to cover up its real purpose. Think about it. They wanted to create a super soldier, but they were smart. The government knew that they couldn't create something like this on Earth. They would need a planet like Earth, but far away from humanity so that they could train and grow this weapon."

Philips lend foreword and tapped on the folder with his index finger. "So Goodwin was going to kill off the crew. He simply just saw us as dispensable workers."

"But you must see it from his point of view. He couldn't have information about this mission leaked throughout the world."

Philips focused the gun's sight in order to reassure his shot. "Then why is he dead?"

Porter smiled at the question. "The government and Colonel Goodwin were merely my pawns. I needed them for the greater picture."

"The greater picture?"

"My creation, of course."

SCATTERED

Meanwhile, the cockpit still held the scientists captive and continued to grow even more anxious. Not one of them sat down in the cockpit, they were all scattered. Rodriguez smoked a cigarette while she lend against the wall. This habit was her fixation when things became stressful. As she placed the rolled paper to her lips, she inhaled the burnt tobacco. From there, she sucked the smoke deep into her lungs where it sat for a moment before she released it. The exhaled smoke floated around her head and began to make its way to the nostrils of Zuckerman. Zuckerman, standing close, looked directly at Rodriguez and she looked back to him.

"You want one?" Rodriguez asked.

Zuckerman smiled, almost revealing the little personality he had. "Haven't you heard? I quit."

Rodriguez held out the package of cigarettes and presented it so that one of the sticks poked its top higher than the others. Zuckerman grabbed the cigarette and placed a portion in his mouth. There was something about the gentle touch of the white sticks on his lips that sent a tranquil feeling through him. Rodriguez lighting it for him was simply icing on the cake, per se.

"These things will be the death of me." Zuckerman's concern was mild.

"I would rather die from this than from a lot of other things."

The cynical joke was badly timed. The reason being was that it had taken away from the serenity of their smoke break. Essentially, it was a buzz kill. However, it would not be the last. Their conversation, though brief, ended at the sound of Thatcher stomping around the cockpit like a child who had not received a desired toy.

"This is ridiculous," Thatcher exclaimed.

Rodriguez watched Thatcher make his way across the cockpit and towards the two. He marched with authority that developed gradually through his impatience and fear.

"We have no idea what is happening on this ship." Thatcher was an arm's length from the two. "Why are we cooped up in this goddamn room?"

A flick of the finger sent Rodriguez cigarette to the floor beneath her. With her foot, she placed its ball on the lighted stick and pivoted. One last breath exhaled from her lungs creating one last cloud of grey haze. She watched the cloud fade and Thatcher's face clarify.

"Look over there," she said, pointing to Watkins's still body. "Is that not enough proof that there is something deadly aboard this ship?"

Thatcher rolled his eyes and harshly sighed. "Come on Rodriguez, do you seriously believe Philips's ghost story?"

The story of these creatures had not been directly told by Philips. Dover had told the scientist of Philips's report upon his first encounter.

"I don't know." Rodriguez chose not to side. "I just know that there are at least three crew members who are dead."

"If these so-called creatures are real, then why haven't any of us seen them?" Thatcher methodically motioned it as he spoke.

"Are you suggesting Philips would make-up something like this?"

"I'd love to ask him about it, but he isn't here right now. In fact, we heard the story from Dover who isn't here either."

"What's your point?"

"My point is that I want answers."

She searched the room scanning with her eyes. She stopped once she found what she was looking for and walked over to a nearby table. On the table were scattered headsets.

"Here," she said picking up one of headsets and placing it in her ear. "We can try and contact them." She pushed a button. "Come in Philips, Come in Dover." A few seconds passed. "Can anyone hear me? I repeat, come in Philips. Come in Dover!"

Rodriguez looked at Zuckerman and the two stared at each other blankly. She looked back to Thatcher, who stood with his arms crossed and his foot tapping the hard floor. If Thatcher's smirk was not enough to express his precision, then his tapping was reassuring.

"No answer, huh?" he bragged.

"Something isn't right," she exclaimed as she speedily walked to Dover's prized screens. "Communications must be down on ship."

Before she could approach the screens, she realized that they were blank. She stopped and stared at the pilot stations. The screens lacked the colorful luminance and maneuverability of earlier. No holographic display, just the two unmanned stations.

"Avi!" Her call was unanswered. "No communication and no vessel intelligence, they are both out." She focused on Thatcher.

Thatcher ran his hand through his hair.

"I think I'll take my chances."

Rodriguez walked over to Thatcher and placed her hand on his shoulder. Thatcher turned away, brushing her hand from his arm. A protective gesture by her; however, it was undesired. Making his way to the exit, he found a handgun and picked it from its table. Firearms were never his specialty, but he had a general idea of their workings.

"Thatcher, don't do this. Stay here where it is safe."

Rotating back to the other two, he explained his motives. "I am going to figure this out for myself. I don't need any more ghost stories."

Zuckerman stepped forward and walked over to Thatcher. Although he had been nearly lifeless during the interaction, he made his presence now known.

"Zuckerman?" Rodriguez hoped to change his mind.

"We can't let him go out there by himself," Zuckerman followed.

"Yes, and what if Philips was telling the truth? What if there really are these creatures? You both will die."

Zuckerman and Rodriguez held a stare between each other. Her eyes were weary, for she wished they would not take this unnecessary risk. Thatcher, on the other hand, had ignored Rodriguez completely. He continued to the door with his back facing her. Like a mother calling for her child, Zuckerman read Thatcher's continuance as such and followed. Zuckerman neglected to grab a weapon, but exited the cockpit standing behind Thatcher's protection. With one last glance over his shoulder, the two were gone.

Frustrated with the two's ignorant decisiveness, Rodriguez ripped the headset from her ear. Compactly, she tossed it onto the floor. It hit the floor hard and shattered into multiple pieces of plastic and wires. She lowered her head away from the cockpit's door, after it closed completely. In this action, her eyes discovered the pieces of the headset. Partially indicative it was. There the scattered piece laid, dysfunctional with their unity broken. Inevitably, the headset could not be fixed, for it now was destroyed.

IN THE EYE OF THE BEHOLDER

Philips had not lost the sharp aim he held on Porter. Despite the firearm pointed in his face, Porter did not confess because he felt its threatening presence. Instead, it was almost as if he welcomed it so that he could flaunt his creation. Hiding nothing, Porter now invited virtually every question Philips could conjure.

"What was your plan, Porter?" Philips asked. "To exploit the government for its funding and then claim the result for yourself?"

Porter chuckled in his seat at the simplistic explanation that Philips presented. From his pocket, he pulled his coin and set his forearms on the table's flat surface. Deterring away from Philips briefly, he took out a coin and placed it on the surface. He let the item stand while holding on to it. With a flick of his thumb and index finger, the coin spun. It spun at a constant speed, which was enough to draw Philips's eyes. A few rotations passed before Philips recognized how he had become mesmerized. Eliciting his amazement, he continued to watch it until it wobbled. For the first time, he examined the coin for the image that was on its face. The slower it spun the more detail he could see until the coin came to a complete rest.

On its face was a golden, carved beast, standing on all fours. The beast held a strong base with its chest and its bovine snout raised high. The horns atop its head gave him the conclusion that it was a bull. Not a typical image for a coin; however, Porter seemed to worship the coin, for he always had it within his reach.

Swiftly, Philips's attention was snapped due to Porter's brisk hand motion. Porter relocated the coin to his palm and left the table spot bare. With Philips's eyes fixed on the spot, Porter spoke. "Yes, actually, in a way, that is exactly what I did." Porter did not find Philips's questions insulting. "But I didn't want my creation to be a soldier. My heart was set on something else. I wanted perfection."

The word returned without Philips mentioning it. Porter had addressed it for him. However, this time Philips had fingered out the answers to his questions, for it was now clear. Each detail seemed to piece its way together like a puzzle so that he could now see the greater picture.

"Perfection," Philips spoke with vigor in his tone. "Your creature is your perfection?"

"Yes, Lieutenant." He paused. "My perfect race."

"How is *this* the perfect race?"

"Physically, they are perfect. I created a virus that carried the genetic make-up for all the most beneficial traits I could brainstorm. See, a virus does one of two things, it either replicates itself and kills off the other cells of an organism or it mutates the cell. See, I have developed a virus that does both, so that it gets the benefits of both."

Philips listened but was growing angry at Porter's blindness to the situation. He wanted to find the answers that he so desperately pursued; however, he was also very interested in Porter's explanation.

"When I paired the virus with a fresh organism, the organism recognizes the virus as part of itself. The cells replicate at substantial rates, while the virus passes the genetic material from cell to cell. As a result the organism grows and develops at record speeds—with its perfect genes, of course." He rephrased himself in layman's term so that Philips could fully grasp his concept of perfection. "Essentially, these creatures evolve faster, are physically stronger, and in time they could be smarter than any human."

"But they are dangerous to us. Your creatures are killing us." Philips's frustration continued. "What you are doing is no different than what Goodwin planned to do."

"You are wrong, Lieutenant! I gave you the chance to live and you all choose to attack my creation. Because of this, the creatures see you and the others as a threat to their survival. What is the only way to get rid of a threat? To kill it off, of course."

"So they will kill you as well?"

Porter cracked a grin. "They see me for what I am. I am their creator. I am the one who nurtured them and gave them life. They won't kill me. In fact, quite the opposite. In time, they will actually learn to worship me."

"Worship you? Why create something like this to begin with?" Philips lowered his head. "What are you trying to prove?"

Porter changed the subject. "Let me ask you something Philips," he began. "If God is perfect and he created us in his image, then why are humans not perfect?" Porter did not allow for Philips to answer. "Because, there is no god. It is merely an image, something people hope for. If there was a god, there would be no imperfections."

Philips stopped and sighed. "This isn't about God, this about you proving something to yourself."

He was attempting to spark aggression from the seemingly calm scientist. Porter expressed an emotionless exterior, but Philips saw past it. He knew that no individual could avoid the emotions associated with the tragedies of life. One could deny it and bury their pain deep within their core. Nonetheless, the emotion is always there. The trick for Philips was to find the catalyst to its release. With this goal and an idea, he continued.

"I can understand the pain you are experiencing." Porter rose from his chair, interrupting the slightly startled Philips. He stayed behind the safety of his weapon. Porter turned away from table and made his way to the corner of the rectangular room. The table still separated the two, but Philips's aim held a new angle over its surface. Watching down the barrel, he peered sharply at Porter's backside, waiting for him to rebuttal. But peculiarly, he stayed silent. From the view of his backside, Philips worked his sight to Porter's hand. In his hand, the polished gold coin peaked its top from Porter's fingers. He did not rotate the piece nor did he move it. The coin stayed perfectly still.

"I can understand the pain you are experiencing." Philips repeated, preparing his next dagger.

"The loss of your wife and unborn child," Philips finished. He had found the coffin that was buried underneath the dirt of Porter's grave. An apparent victory as Porter gradually turned and faced him. Porter's face was blank, but Philips could see the fire in his eyes—a hatred that was not directed at Philips; instead, a hatred directed elsewhere. Porter opened his mouth and delivered his testimony.

"You can understand my pain? Don't taunt me, Lieutenant. You know nothing of the pain I've endured." Porter condemned Philips with his words. "To have your family stripped from you while you helplessly try to save them."

Porter walked around the table causing Philips to turn his aim. He got closer and closer to Philips until the gun was nearly touching his skull. Philips held the gun with a deathly grip, awaiting any sudden motions.

"Nar." Philips felt that the name would calm him slightly. "I've seen death up close. I know what it does to people. You're letting your pain fuel even greater pain. Please, we can end this now."

"Why would I want to end this? I have achieved creation. I have created a physically perfect being. Something that no god could have ever done."

Surprisingly, Philips felt sympathy for him at this moment. He just wished that Porter would see the consequences of his creation. Here was a man who was not evil and was not insane, but a man that was driven by passion. A passion that was caused by pain and a pain that came from thievery hands of fate. He had had all he ever loved taken from him by the imperfections of the world. Oddly, Philips understood his intentions, but they were not solely righteous enough to justify his creation. Still, now that the mystery was unraveling, Philips needed to cure Porter's blindness. Philips believed he could convince Porter of his mistake.

"Don't you see? This creation of yours is completely subjective. What you see as perfect might not be perfect in the eyes of someone else."

Porter was irritated with Philips's inability to side with him; however, Philips continued.

"This is simply a case of transference. You wanted to successfully create life, seeing that your child was taken from you before its birth." Philips was attempting a tough approach to shake Porter into realization. "But, it wasn't enough to stop there. Disease, one of the many physical flaws. Seeing that your wife died from a disease, you sought to create something that wouldn't repeat the same fate. Then you took it a step further. You conjured up this idea that you would make something that was immune to the physical imperfections of the world. However, you can't. There will always be some kind of imperfection. There will always be some form of evil."

Philips stopped and looked down for a moment. He looked at his boots as they staggered themselves on the room's level, white floor. But it was not his boots or the floor that had pulled him away from speech. It was his own thought—no, more than a thought, a realization of his own. For first time since before his time in the military, there was a new light. He thought about what he had said and though it was a cynical comment, it was the truth. But this was a truth, where deep below its exterior it held a sense of goodness. For an extended period in his life he had lost his faith because of the evils in the world, something he himself sought to get rid of. Ironically, once he had seen the action attempted—through Porter's so-called perfection—he felt differently.

Abruptly, Porter began to speak again. Though Philips digressive thought closed for the moment, it would stay with him.

"Are you finished, Lieutenant?" Porter's tone was sharp and strict.

Philips looked up at Porter. Just by the expression of his face, Philips could tell that he had not convinced the other party in the room. Porter obviously did not want to hear anymore of Philips's effort. He would not stand for Philips's attempt to beat him in his own mind games.

"You know I truly hoped to convince you myself," Porter said. "But now you stand in my way. I will not be denied of this, Lieutenant."

"Please, Porter. Stop this before it goes too far. The entire crew will die."

"Does that bother you, Lieutenant?"

"Does what bother me?"

"The fact that the crew will die." Porter broke his elongated seriousness with a smile. "It appears as though it doesn't."

"What do you mean?"

"You stand here and debate with me while they die."

Philips was confused of where Porter was headed.

"They're safe, at the moment," Philips countered. "They're all in the same place. Besides I would have known if someone had left because Avi would have told me."

"Are you sure of this, Lieutenant?" Porter's smirk continued. "Maybe you should check and see."

Philips reached for his headset but kept the handgun straight in his opposite hand. He pressed its button and tested.

"Avi?" There was no response so he tried once more. "Avi?" A louder tone, but the same result.

Porter continued to eye Philips with a smile of dramatic irony. However, Philips, on the other hand, stayed persistent and changed the frequency.

"Come in, Dover."

Nothing.

"Come in. Can anybody hear me?"

Dead silence.

Realizing that the ship's communications were down, Philips lowered his hand from his headset and reverted to Porter. His sympathy for the man had faded, while his previous anger returned.

"What did you do, Porter?"

"Let's just say we will not be returning to Earth."

"What did you do, Porter?"

"You didn't honestly believe that Goodwin and Dover were the only two that knew of the virus, did you?"

"The computer virus?" Philips dismissed the idea. "Even if you had applied it to Avi, Dover can still override it."

"True, but that's if he is still alive."

Philips lowered his gun as his heart sank. This thought terrified him, for it represented the recognition that the return to Earth was nearly impossible. He back away from Porter slowly, navigating his backside first. A further hidden agenda was divulging itself, but there was too much for Philips's to grasp. His thoughts rushed through his head causing him to fall into an endless spiral. He felt the overwhelming burden of responsibility. He felt the responsibility to protect the crew, the responsibility to return home to his wife and son, the responsibility to expose the truth, but most of all the responsibility to end this nightmare. Continuing to back pedal, he contemplated putting a bullet through Porter's head, but realized this action would not suffice any purpose. Porter was merely a man who desired reparations for the pain he borne. Even so, Philips was no murder nor would Porter's death destroy the creatures that were procreating aboard.

The door was met and it parted allowing for Philips to shift from the room to the residential corridor. As the doors closed upon his exit, the spacing between them provided just enough. With his front still facing the inside of the room, he observed Porter for a final few seconds. He had not moved an inch and neither did his crooked smile. Just for that brief moment, Philips felt a tingling through his body and slightly question his previous decision. However, the thought vanished as so did the image Porter. Before Philips was a blank door and behind him was an empty hall, possibly awaiting his final search.

WHAT FATE MAY HOLD

What fate held for Philips and the others seemed potentially dark. However, it would not wait for the future to expose itself. It made the empty, white hallway feel colder and much more condensed. He had never been much of a claustrophobic, but the constant necessity of checking every angle contributed to the partial phobia. With numerous thoughts on his mind, he tried to clear them. Seeing the environment was enough to worry about, he could not afford to think of anything else.

Philips stopped in his tracks, thinking he heard movement. As he approached an upcoming one-way turn in the hallway, he exchanged the handgun for the rifle on his back. The handgun found his waistline, while the rifle found his shoulder. He held the rifle pointed for a moment, then tucked it into his chest and took cover behind the corner separating the halls. Slowing his breathing was the best way to ensure his current covert affair; however, he needed an idea of what he was potentially up against. With this ensuing thought, he noticed a little space between him and the corner. But it was just enough to possibly give him a better look. His foot slid closer to the corner and the muscles in his calves tensed, pulling his top-heavy physic. Once the motion was complete, his body was in the perfect position to allow him to observe. He poked from around the corner, one facial feature at a time until his entire head surpassed. As he turned the corner fully, a shadowy figure appeared across the floor, causing him to raise his rifle with force. He glowered down the top of the rifle, neglecting the scope. His heart raced, but as his vision adjusted he was able to see. With a sigh, he lowered the rifle.

"Jesus, Philips!" The woman exclaimed.

"What are you doing out of the cockpit?" Philips was protective like a worrisome parent.

"Is this how you greet people? With a rifle pointed to their face?"

Philips ignored her sarcasm. "Where are the others?"

"I went to find them. I tried to stop them from leaving, but they were so insistent on finding out for themselves."

"Damn it."

"What's going on, Philips?"

"I don't know how much time we have Rodriguez."

"Time for what, Philips? I want to know what you know."

Philips pulled the handgun from his waistline and held it in front of him. He held its barrel, grip side and trigger presented for Rodriguez. She placed her hand on the gun and softly pulled it from his grip.

"Come on," Philips said, casting a gentle breeze as he passed by her. "We can't stand here in the open, we have to keep moving."

Rodriguez followed him, despite his inability to answer her question. She thought about asking again; however, his focus seemed to be on the walk ahead of them. In a slightly crouched position, Philips slowly walked down the hall with his rifle ready. Rodriguez followed behind him a few steps, gingerly holding her own weapon to her side. The distant between them and the end of hall was decreasing to where they could fully see the lack of detail of the halls end. This specific strip was just the first of their travels. The two maneuvered through a series of similar corridors, with obviously no apparent definition. After a while of walking, Rodriguez began to grow anxious. The idea loomed that Philips had still neglected to divulge any information.

"You still haven't answered me, Philips."

He looked back at her inquisitive face. He had not been ignoring Rodriguez because he refused to inform her, rather he was focused on the impending potential for danger. From her tranquil approach to their travel, he could sense her ignorance. Surprisingly, she had not seen the creature even once and was completely oblivious to the information Philips had obtained.

"Dr. Porter," he began.

The response was a surprise to her. She did not expect any dialogue during his apparent focus. He held the majority of his attention on the hall.

"I don't understand."

"These creatures, they are his creation."

She remained silent causing Philips to turn and recognize her desire to understand.

"This mission wasn't for exploration Rodriguez." He captured her full attention. "We were being used."

"For what?"

"For war... For creation... For the satisfaction of others."

Rodriguez grabbed Philips by the arm causing him to stop and face her. As he looked at her he could see the confused expression.

"What are you talking about, Philips?" Rodriguez's tone became increasingly louder.

"Rodriguez, I understand that you are extremely confused right now, but we can't stay here. These creatures, they don't wait for clarification. They want one thing, and that's to get rid of us."

She did not seem fazed by his warnings and was seemingly stuck on her comprehension of Philips's explanation. Philips began walking again causing Rodriguez to follow swiftly.

"Where are we going?"

"We have to get to the nuclear room. We have to find Dover."

"And what of the others?"

"They can wait. Without Dover we all share the same fate. Without Dover no one can return home."

There was an extreme amount of confusion between the two; however, Philips recognized this detail as an inappropriate time to explain. This search was almost a matter of life and death. They needed to find Dover. They need to find a way to escape, a way to survive. They walked with a fluid pace, passing through the whiteness of each hall. There was no sound and no sign of life, just merely the eccentric hurry that the two expressed. Directional signs throughout the halls showed that the nuclear room was near, but they would prove themselves to be unnecessary. As they turned a corner furtively, Philips noticed a dark image on the floor ahead of them. He slowed their speed to a creep and pointed his rifle toward the object. The closer he got to the object the clearer it became until he spotted a bold, red streak. The streak was relatively long and thick, stretching itself from the wall to the center of the floor. His sight followed it to the object and with a great force of realization he pushed into an abrupt sprint. He sprinted as fast as he could, with his rifle bounced from its strap. Rodriguez, recognizing the same image, followed at a comparable pace. However, despite their speed, they were too late.

Philips fell to his knees and rolled the dead weight, only to find that his chance of escape had died as well. Rodriguez stood over the two, as Philips placed the side of his head to Dover's chest. He listened hard, but his torso gave Philips nothing but a blood stained ear. In defeat, Philips fell to his rear where he wiped the dark, red from his head. A great sense of a dismal fear now clouded not only the hall but the entire ship. The living two breathed heavily and at an unsystematic rhythm.

"What now?" Rodriguez said with an even greater sense of confusion.

"I don't know." Philips responded.

He bent down and pried the handgun away from Dover's cold, stiff grip. With the handgun securely in a grip of his own, he tucked it tightly into his waistline. Seeing that he was unsure of what the further corridors would hold, he thought an extra weapon might suffice. Deep down, Philips knew that their chance of returning home was nearly impossible. However, his impending thought was to change as something attracted his auditory sense.

The sound was consistent, echoing through the hallways through short, compact series. It popped and banged like an explosion at a small proportion. Philips recognized this sound and knew that with its instance came a threat.

"Did you hear that?" Philips looked through the halls with a feeling of artifice.

"Thatcher and Zuckerman," she mumbled under her breath.

Philip's rifle found its intend position, as it had before, and Philips began to move at a silent trot. Rodriguez followed with somewhat of a bounding skip, but enough to maintain an unintentional distance between her and Philips. They left Dover's body to decay upon the cold floor as they made their way to the end of a proceeding corridor. Seeing that their intent on survival was greater than their respect, the sound ahead presented itself as a priority. Checking the safety of the hall, he followed the sense down the direction of its source. The same popping sounded again, correcting them to the proper direction. The sound continued for one last series and abruptly ended.

"Where are they?" Rodriguez caught up to Philips.

Philips did not respond, but continued to migrate down the empty hallway. He looked to the right and the left of the hall and noticed a few unfamiliar rooms. The rooms appeared to be empty, with no visible light peering through the small windows upon the automated doors. He looked away from the rooms and further down the hall. Appropriate to the maze they found themselves aboard, Philips spotted an adjacent hall. He approached the corner of the wall with caution and stopped at a new sound.

The sound continued to grow. They could both hear it clearly. It hissed like a snake drawing them to its Garden of Eden. But, Philips was wise, holding his ground. The sound then morphed into an elegant and rhythmic clicking, something he hand been in the presence of before. Knowing this familiar form of language, he began to grow weary of it source. With a slight rattle in his hand, he raised his palm so that it faced Rodriguez. She froze.

"What?" She asked, noticing his obvious fear of the emergent sound.

"We need to leave, now." He whispered.

"I don't understand."

"Now."

Philips slowly pushed Rodriguez backwards with his creeping motion. They kept their front sides facing the adjacent hallway. They awaited any threat that may expose itself. Easily they slid through their previous passage way. Philips looked over his shoulder briefly to find one of the doors he had noticed before.

"Here." Philips pointed to their right.

Rodriguez focused fully on opening the door, while Philips's attention strongly held the protection. Her hand located the key pad next to the door and her thumbs leaped from all of its angles. She watched as the key pad chimed and the red light circled in the center of the door changed to green. As it opened, she tapped Philips on the shoulder. The action reacted with him turning and following her into the room. The door closed behind Philips; however, the parted doors thwacked a subtle sound of colliding metal—loud enough to resonate its clap through the precedent and adjacent corridors.

Not knowing about the echoing evidence that had reverberated in the room's exterior, Philips and Rodriguez inspected the room. The inspection began upon Rodriguez turning on the lighting via switch. At first, Philips was not staggered by the room's appearance considering it shared almost an identical shape and white hue as the others. But as he examined it further, he recognized its difference. Upon the walls were counters with utensils stacked on top of them. In the middle of the room, there were a series tables that Philips assumed served the purpose of laying down patients.

The tables were lined up perfectly, with four to a column and two to a row. He counted off the tables in his head and looked off the back few. Stretching from corner to corner, the back wall of the room was lined with all the machines that seemed necessary for surgery and radiology. An infirmary, he concluded. However, the room undoubtedly had no purpose because their deaths were predetermined and the only relatively qualified doctor aboard had his own intensions. If they had known about this room earlier, a few lives could have been saved. Either way, this room was now irrelevant. The damage had been done; therefore, at this moment it was now a place to hide and nothing more.

Philips and Rodriguez split the room evenly, with him to the left and her to the right. Immediately, Rodriguez made her way to the medical supplies that covered the walls and counters. Though she tried to stay silent, the utensils were simply made-up of the wrong material for muteness. Before Philips began his work on his side, he gave Rodriguez a stern look. She embarrassingly gleamed across the room following her clumsiness and acknowledged his hint at silence. On the other hand, Philips led the end of his rifle down the rows of the tables to ensure their safety. He checked the first row, clear. He checked the second, same result. On the third, the row was clear; however, he could feel an uncomfortable object being shoved just below his neck. Even through his uniform, he could feel the chilled touch as it unremitting dug into his vertebrate.

"Turn!" a voice commanded.

The utterance had caught the attention of Rodriguez who snapped her own weapon in its direction. Philips slowly did as the voice instructed. He felt the cool sensation fade as the object revert from his backside. The face of a supposed friend was revealed upon Philips dramatic rotation.

"Zuckerman," Philips identified. "Are you all right?"

He did answer, but elevated his aim so that the handgun was pointed to Philips's forehead.

"Tell Rodriguez to lower her weapon."

Zuckerman spotted her aim from the corner of his eye.

"Please, Zuckerman," Philips said calmly.

"Tell her to lower the damn gun, Philips!"

The only party that was not unsettled by Zuckerman's shout was Zuckerman. Both Philips and Rodriguez were sure that if their previous rambunctiousness did not attract the creature's attentions, then Zuckerman surely would.

"Zuckerman, we need you to calm down right now. We are not any threat to you."

"I swear to God I will put this bullet into your head if she doesn't lower her gun."

The anxiety and apprehension of the ship had become personified by Zuckerman. Undoubtedly, he had been driven by his instincts to protect himself and only himself. Fear of the unknown had caused him to turn on his friends. He blinked harshly as he struggled to hold the gun as it wobbled in Philips's face.

"Where's Thatcher?" Philips asked.

"Those things."

"It's okay now, we are here to help. Please lower the weapon Zuckerman."

"They followed you didn't they?" Zuckerman chocked his gun. "You brought them to me."

"Don't lower your gun, Rodriguez." Philips instructed.

"I should shoot you both right now!"

"Damn it, Philips! He is going to shoot." Rodriguez returned with a soft voice that held enough power to be heard clearly.

"Trust me," Philips ensured.

Zuckerman glared deeply into Philips's eyes guiding energies of his fear. Philips stayed calm sensing the fretfulness through Zuckerman's bloodshot eyes. The room was deathly still, but a climactic result was afoot.

"Philips!"

Before Zuckerman could gather the nerve to pull the trigger, Philips snatched the barrel of the gun. The two both held a firm grip on the gun, but Philips's strength was enough to force Zuckerman's aim away. The struggle caused him to dimly discharge three bullets into the ground. Overpoweringly, Philips's stronghold upon the weapon allowed him to throw his elbow into Zuckerman's face. He harshly fell to the ground, holding his delicately shattered nose. The blood rushed from his nose and through the cracks of his fingers. Philips stood and watched as Zuckerman fought to gather himself to a four-limbed position. For insurance purposes, he held the newly acquire pistol on his pugnacious crewmember. This threat was short-lived.

From the entrance of the room came a loud banging. His attention reverted itself back to the door where Philips could see the banging through the vibration. Everyone in the room saw the door continuously rattle while there was no doubt in any of their minds what was on the other side. A furious screech triggered a response of Philips quickly bending and grabbing the bloodied Zuckerman by the arm. He pulled him close and threw him behind an operating table in the far left of the room. Without hesitation, Rodriguez expressed the same idea, ducking her way behind the table on the far right side. Philips concealed the handgun and traded it for the rifle that hung from the strap on his shoulder. He gestured the notion of silence to both with his index finger placed upon his lips. He slid next to Zuckerman's left and established cover.

The banging was persistent and continued to grow louder. Multiple screeches began to accumulate giving Philips no disbelief that there was more than one. The real fear that laid with in him was how many creatures were on the other side. With its loudest bang, the door split down its middle seem. The screeches were now directly clear with no sound barrier between them. The banging transitioned to a tearing as the creatures ripped through the metal. They were in the room.

"Stay calm," Philips said in a whisper to Zuckerman.

Zuckerman shook profusely, rattling his back against the table. Philips placed his hand across his chest to settle his tension; however, Zuckerman's fear was too great to withhold. Their steps were prominent like a hunter crushing the shrubs in a forest. The clicking and popping of their language bounced back and forth between however many there were. Using his sense of echolocation, Philips was able to identify where they were in the room. He shifted his hand to Zuckerman's arm and dragged him to the left side of the table. They stayed put for a moment and with his senses they moved once again; this time to the proceeding table. Philips leaned over him and peaked around the table's rear to see if Rodriguez had moved as well. Instead, a thin, beige leg clouded his vision causing him to snap back to his cover. The creature screeched once more, filling their human ears with the sound of pain-struck swine.

The creature moved over to the opposite side of the table, hop in its step. The two men could sense the creature presence residing over them. Its breath was slow, yet heavy. Philips could feel the warmth gusting over his head methodically. The situation was all too similar, but he knew this time his fortune would not be as great. Looking at Zuckerman was the telltale sign of what was to come, for he lacked the stomach that Philips had possessed. He quivered with every sequenced puff of the hot air. Despite the heat, Zuckerman's skin was icy, while his forehead moisturized itself with small droplets. He was a time-bomb and his panting was merely the ticking of the clock. The creature could sense his fear and was toying with the emotion.

Philips eyed Zuckerman's fist clenching itself upon the cool floor. He went to grab a hold of his sleeve to maintain his composure, but it was too late. Zuckerman had flung himself out in the open, compromising not only himself but the others as well. Holding his position, Philips watched as the creature leaped across the table and slammed Zuckerman to the ground. Relentlessly, it threw its arms onto his helpless body. The others followed suit, ganging on him like a group of thugs. Philips listened as their cries mashed together, one of pain and the other of aggression. Knowing that his discovery was forthcoming, he compactly sprang to a crouch and slipped around the opposite side.

"Rodriguez! Run!" He hollered.

His voice triggered a reaction from the other creatures while Rodriguez raised her body and ran to the entrance. Realizing his crouch would not be suitable for speed, he rose to full extension and caught a glimpse of the others. The others' attention pulled away from Zuckerman and to the rising Philips. By this time Rodriguez was already distant, gliding past the demolished doorway. Philips gathered a brief head count of the creatures. His adrenaline blurred the ability to count precisely. Four, maybe five, was his tentative number. Nonetheless, he knew the number did not matter; either number would force an immediate escape.

Philips pushed himself away from the table beside him and slid his way throughout the proceeding tables. From behind him, the creatures continued to let out their high-pitched squeals. As deathly and frightening as they were, they only seemed to cause Philips to run faster and harder. When his bouncing through the tables was complete, he jumped through the door way. With a glimpse across his shoulder, he saw the creatures making their way through the maze. He fired his rifle in their direction in hopes of slowing them; though, their pace was only slightly halted. They leaped through and across the tables at a much more powerful and efficient rate. All four of their limbs touched the ground, like wild felines hunting their pray.

"Philips!" Rodriguez cried from further down the corridor.

"Keep running!" Philips yelled as he turned toward her direction.

He slid a little across the dry, marble-like floor. His boots must have lacked the sticky consistence needed to hold a powerful foot plant. He ignored the sleekness of his equipment and regained his footing. The unit pursued behind the frantically sprinting Philips, but surprisingly Philips held his distance. He turned and fired a round of bullets with the rifle in one hand while sprinting forward. A few of his bullets pierced the resistant skin of one of the creatures causing it to stumble and tumble over its shoulder. He looked at the creatures roll head first, and turned back to fluid running form.

Neither Philips nor Rodriguez knew to where they were headed. They simply ran for the fear of their lives. In some sense, Rodriguez led the way seeing that Philips remained in route behind her. However, her destination was soon predetermined with a dead end approaching. The only option was a sharp turn left down another unsurprising twist and turn that the ship had provided for the crew. She was the only one who could see down the contiguous lane, for Philips still trailed in the previous hall.

Rodriguez's new direction was short and one dimensional. At the end, there was what seemed to be a large gate-like door that permitted entry by parting into the hallway's parallel walls. Conveniently, she recognized that the lighting in the center of the door was green. She did not dwell on the thought. She needed to find the opening mechanism. As she ran, her vision bounced; however, she tried to search for a level or a key pad. Her eyes bounced around the grey door like a bounding rubber ball. The yellow trim around the outside of the door met at the top and bottom, forming an octagon. It was split down the center from its intended point of separation. Knowing the details of the door were useless by the time she arrived in front of the door. There she stood without a clue of how this gate opened. In desperation, she then looked to the right wall and found it.

"Philips!" She screamed as she made her way to the key pad. "I found a door."

Philips had heard her but did not respond. With the creatures nearly grazing at his heels, their vocal gestures were eating away at his hopes of survival. He made it to the contiguous lane. The sleekness of his boots sent him to the ground, but his left hand found the floor, saving him from the fall. Pulling away from the floor, he could see that Rodriguez had programmed the universal code into the wall. The door opened at a gradual pace and Philips pushed his hand hard. Returning to a sprint, he glanced again. He watched as three of creatures clumsily struggled with their footing as well. They slid passed the hall, exiting his visibility.

"Hurry!" Rodriguez had made her way onto the other side.

Suddenly, a fourth appeared behind the others. This creature was smarter and handled the turn with ease. It quickly changed its direction towards the humans, but oddly it stopped. It stood at the end of the hall for a moment, eyeing down its prey. Almost a taunt of some sort, it held its humanoid stance. Gathering itself briefly, the beast fell to all fours and with a flip of the switch it charged. Not only was the creature pursuing at a full attack, but its lust and vitality were rejuvenated.

"Close the door!" Philips could feel its baring presence.

"Not without you!" Rodriguez returned.

"Close the damn door!"

She complied and found the switch that activated the closing mechanism. Though the door was only partially opened, it still closed very slowly. Philips could see the doors sticking from the wall like the teeth in a mouth. The jaws of the wall sent these teeth closer and closer as Philips got closer and closer to the door. Fatigue was slowing him, while the creature seemed to gain endurance and force with every low-lined gallop. He could hear the creature's breathing, feeling its intensity and fire upon his backside. However, he was nearing his safety at the same time. Philips leaped through mouth and into the stomach of the room. He hit the ground hard, on the other side, crashing the muscular padding of his shoulder. He tumbled just above the white floor's glossy surface and landed on his back, gliding just a few yards.

Philips quickly faced the door and immediately knew they were not yet safe. He took a knee and whipped his rifle around to his shoulder; the strap enabled a smooth swing. The crack between the door grew tighter as so did Philips aim. Violently the creature flew through the opening, clipping its arm against a side. The door caused it to bleed; however, it did not hinder its attack. It skidded across the floor by its hands and feet and hurdled itself at Philips in one apparent motion. Philips returned fire across the creatures flesh as it soared through the air. A few bullets punctured, but a few was not enough to prevent it. It cascaded Philips to the ground causing him to wince fervidly. Every bone in his torso's side seemed to crack upon the impact. He let out a passionate scream to express the shredding pain and anguish. He gripped the source while the creature attempted to finish its work. With his boot, he supplied the only forcible solution and his leg pushed the creature back. He released his grip and found his rifle once more. A few more bullets escaped the chamber before the clip went dry. He was doomed by the grasps of death— nothing to prevent it, only the temporary safety provided by the extension of his leg and the padded sole of his boot. Keeping his leg angled as barrier, he closed his eyes.

An ear-splitting crackle echoed through the room like a single firework exploding into the night sky. The creature fell heavily onto the chest of Philips causing him to forcibly grunt. Once he had regained the air in his lungs, he opened his eyes to find the creature still. Its red fluid ran, seeping from its wounds and onto Philips's uniform. In noticeable pain, he rolled the creature to his side where it rested on its back. Heavy due to its dead weight, he relaxed as he examined it further. Upon its apparent temple resided an oozing hole about the size of a bullet. He turned away from the creature to find Rodriguez standing ncxt to a closed door shaking. In her hand, she held the aim of a modified handgun. With one final sigh, Philips fell to his back. He closed his eyes and slowly escaped the thrashing pain. Gradually, it faded away until it was completely masked by the relaxation of a deeply, slowed heart rate.

HE KNOWS NOT WHAT HE HAS DONE

The view from the balcony was magnificently portrayed like a completed canvas surrounding him. Lushes hills had replaced the ants and their construction, leaving nothing but untouched land. He stared out onto the waved banks and watched the lowering sun delicately kiss their crowns. As he surveyed this elegant sunset, he rested on the cool, metal railing before his chest. His heart matched that of the scenery, beating softly but enough to keep his breath. From his face he felt the warm, placid touch of a kiss upon his cheek. He turned to find its source. Behind him was a pair of baby, blue eyes that seemed to further feed warmth and tenderness into his soul. His love's golden hair gently floated like a feather in the wind, while he stroke a few strands from her face to the back of her head. He looked down to find a small child cradled by her milky forearms and pressed against her elegant, green sun dress. Wrapped in a blanket of soft cotton, the baby poked its small head just enough to see its mother. Its face gleamed, as it too had become lost in her gorgeous sky-filled eyes. It was hard to not be drawn, he related, appreciating the innocents of his new born. With his hand, he caressed the child's smooth and untouched forehead.

The moment was solidified. It was his. It captured his entire being to the point of pure delight. He wished he could live in this scene for the rest of his life; however, deep within himself he knew he had to let go. He knew that some things were imminent. Evil was approaching and it threatened them from a distance. It was something that he could not allow to spread to them, for his wife and child were something he would risk anything to protect. He knew that there would be nothing that would stop him from preventing their pain, their suffering. They were his. They were his life, his perfection. And though it was not ideal, he knew what he needed to do.

The thought was met by a sharp stab to his side abdomen. Both hands found the sight and clenched tightly against it. The pain systematically trekked down each bone of his rib cage as a stick being run across a wooden fence. He grimaced slightly to compensate, but the grimace on his face did not subside. Instead, his wife and child were the ones to fade as he looked up in search of their comfort. As he stretched one arm in their direction and the other gripping the agony, they both seemed to drift farther and farther away. The smile across his wife face continued to distance itself from him. His breath began to escape him while his stretched arm grew weaker from the lack of support. He pulled his hand back to his side and fell to his knees. His vision blurred so he blinked to recover the clarity of her smile. All detail was indistinguishable. Blindness had filled his surrounding with nothing but utter darkness.

"Philips?" A gentle, feminine voice circulated through his head. "Philips?"

His sights slowly separated. He blinked again, but this time he found the steady glow of a white light just above his head. Behind him was a glass wall that supported his neck and back. His legs stretched out before him like a pair of motionless logs. All of his feeling came from the intense agony that culminated throughout his left side. He scrunched his face and forced out a grunted breath.

"You've been out a while," Rodriguez explained.

He moved his head to the side, away from the ceiling, and to his counterpart.

"I found something in the infirmary that might ease your pain a little."

She approached him from the side and knelt just inches away. From her pocket she pulled a handful of short and circular tablet-looking objects. As she held the palm of her hand flat; Philip observed the objects. Five of them filled her hand, but they were small, about the size of a twenty-five cent piece. The tablets had black coverings and what appeared to be a smooth edged cap on one of the sides. She pulled her tanned hand away from his face and returned four to her pocket. She held the individual piece close to her body and flicked its top to the floor. The cap quickly fell to the floor, its plastic consistency skipped around to a rest. His eyes focused on the sharp point that was revealed from underneath the cap. She glanced up at him then back to the drug. Once she had the drug configured, she transferred the tablet to one hand and grabbed his arm with the other. Philips watched her struggle to roll up the tightly conforming material. In an act of graciousness, he aided her in her attempt to uncover his forearm. She turned the inside of his arm over and with one swift jab; she stuck the needle clean into his blood stream.

"I'm sorry." Her action was far from demure, but Philips did not mind the gesture; he had simply hoped to vanquish the impending pain by any means necessary. Rodriguez pulled the needle from the firm tension of his forearm. As she unrolled his sleeve, Philips could feel the warm ecstasy rush through his veins and wrap itself around the pain like a fireproof blanket around a flame. With this newly refurbished sense of peace, he reverted his head back to its rested position against the glass and scanned his surroundings.

The room was relatively short in width, but long in terms of length. He swept the length of the room with his head shifting at a slow and gradual pace. From the door in which they entered through to the back of the room, he saw groups of cells with thick glass separating them from the middle foyer. There was white walling that spaced the sets of glass; though it was minimal. He partially looked over his shoulder and noticed that he had been resting on the same design behind him. Holding cells was his impression, merely the décor of a stylistic prison. He moved back to his front and found the unwelcomed visitor that lifelessly laid across the pale, cold floor. Eyes fixed on the monster, Philips attempted to conjure up a conclusion.

"What is this place?" Rodriguez asked as she sat next to Philips and rested her back against the glass in a similar way.

"I think it is some kind of containment area." Philips's voice was soft and raspy.

Philips turned to Rodriguez. Her sight stayed focused on her kill. Her eyes seemed glazed from pure fear, while her cheeks were a rosy hue from adrenaline. She was still and as motionless as the creature; nevertheless, a symptom of shock.

"I want to know what you know." Surprisingly she spoke.

He held his gaze on Rodriguez and avoided any deviance from the truth.

"We were part of an experiment. Nothing more. Colonel Goodwin was the head of a project to create these creatures. They were going to be his *super soldier.* They knew this planet was habitable, they just needed a way to hide it."

"What happened?"

"Dr. Porter couldn't stand to watch his creation be taken from him so he kept it for himself."

"Where is he now? He's dead right? Those things got him too, right?"

There was a pause between the two. The question seemed best to not be answered. Philips could never admit to Rodriguez that Porter was alive because he neglected to take his life. The fear of losing her trust and the only ally he had was enough motivation for him to conceal the truth.

Conversely, Rodriguez found the pause to be insufficient in limiting her needed wisdom. She continued to ask questions.

"What was his plan?"

"To kill anybody in his way," Philips speculated. "Once we were gone, the creatures will be released. Exodus will be theirs."

To Philips, it was odd that Rodriguez had not questioned his assumptions. Unknowingly, this acceptance was due to the fact that Philips had been right before. Rodriguez was determined to not succumb to the same mistakes that Thatcher had. Her life was much too valuable.

Through her dejected face she asked, "What do we do?"

Philips looked down to the pasty yet glossed floor. He examined the shine from the overhead light's reflection. Thinking of a way to down play the situation would merely create optimism, nothing concrete. Their future was predetermined and return seemed nearly impossible. The reality was that neither of them knew how to reactivate Avi, let alone fly the craft.

"You need to escape."

"Escape?"

"Yes. Neither one of us can fly this ship and a timely rescue just doesn't seem likely."

"But what about you?"

"We can't risk the spread of this creature."

Rodriguez indirectly understood his implications.

"What will you do?" She rephrased.

"What I have to."

"Philips this isn't your fight. We can escape together. Wait for someone to come for us. We have seen this environment, we can survive."

"And risk this contamination on the next people who come to Exodus? Maybe worse." He looked her in the eye. "I've seen these things develop at substantial rates. We don't know what they could become. This must be stopped before humanity is further threatened."

He knew that she could sense the pain that he was experiencing. She blankly stared into his soul and could see the darkness begin to cloud his hopes.

"Then I am coming with you," she insisted.

"No," Philips exclaimed. "You can survive, besides I don't know how much longer I have."

Upon his comment he looked to his side. The simple gesture of looking at his injury helped the drugs fade quickly. Even the slightest motions became unbearable and unmanageable. His breathing was now difficult and inconsistent. Neither wanted to admit to the severity of the injury; however, its reality was that it was potentially fatal.

"You think you could figure out how to fly one of the Hawks?" He continued.

"I don't think I have a choice." Philips eyed her with concern, enabling her to recognize his sincerity.

"...Yes."

"I will give you a head start to get to the bay and find a vehicle."

Philips's final statement was enough to ensure Rodriguez of his full intentions. With a look of remorse upon her face, she pulled her back from the glass and marble based chair and stood. She removed the pistol from the backside of her waist-line and ripped it cocked. Lowering one hand to her side, she turned her body toward Philips. Though she stood before him, her vision was to the floor. The emotion and ambivalence of the situation took away her strength to look him in the eyes. He recognized her level of ambiguity and felt the need to provide further instruction.

"This will all be over soon," he started. "Make sure the hallways are clear. Avoid them at all cost. You make what you think are the safest decisions."

Slowly her head rose from the highly reflective floor and found the intense mien across his eyes. "This evil, Rodriguez. It must be stopped." He spoke further. "Porter doesn't know what he has created. He doesn't see the pain, the suffering that he has caused. I must stop it. I have to do what is right."

ATOP A HILL

Rodriguez turned the corner of the brightly lit corridor and found the door that provided an entrance to the bay. She had not encountered a single creature upon her voyage throughout the hallways, which seemed unlike due to their rapid growth. A small blessing to that point; it was something that gave her dismal hope. As she approached the unopened door way, she breathed at a moderate pace. This action was a trick she had to focus on in order to maintain her limited tranquility. It was partial because of the seemingly never ending travel to her destination. Seeing that every turn she had taken was filled with suspense, minutes were converted to intensive hours.

With just feet left between her and the door, she held out her unarmed hand towards an operating button to the side. The door parted slowly and Rodriguez quickly hit the slightly protuberant wall with her back. Her cover was safe for the moment, so she peel herself from the doors side to better her recognition of the bay. Though the large room appeared empty, an uncanny feeling circulated through her mind. Nevertheless, whether certainty or uncertainty, she had no other choice but to enter with the intention of escaping. Her vision bounded around the room for a moment, simply for her own satisfaction. Then she spotted two things: a Hawk and another key pad. Without vacillation, she took off towards the key pad next to the large, bay door. Once she arrived to the pad, she placed her hands on her knees and began to pant from a hunched position. Realizing her time was miniscule, her body straightened while her fingers programmed a sequence.

A great clashing sound sent the extravagant doorway into opposite directions. The sound was surely enough to attract all attention from any looming beings in the room. However, her focus was not on the sound, but it was towards her absent-mindedness. She had forgotten to put on a suit. Even though the doors continued to part at a dawdling haste, the outside air would fill her lungs before she could line herself with the necessary gear. With faith in their environmental calculations, she took a deep breath. The doors at this point were completely open and her breathing was normal. A sense of excitement filled her for a brief moment, for there had been the revival of the crew's sense of discovery.

Once again, she refocused and spirited to the Hawk she had spotted from her cover. The Exodus air filtered through her lungs rapidly with no distinction from Earth. Confidence filled her thoughts, with freedom and safety looming in the balance. She hit the Hawk at full running speed, putting up her hand against its side to ease her impact. Her free hand found a latch on the pilot's door and pulled so that the door lifted to the ceiling. She tossed her pistol to the passenger's seat then she settled her backside into her own seat. With a hard thrust, she pulled the door towards her allowing it to lock in place.

Abruptly, there was a loud thump atop the vehicle. The sound caused Rodriguez to partially leap from her seat. Her heart began to race while she scurried for her handgun, leaning over the console. Her hand met the weapon while she peered around the craft for any sight of life. As she tried to grip the firearm it slipped farther from her grip to the floor board. Her lack of attention took away from her eye-hand coordination. Panicking further, she disregarded the weapon and returned to the Hawk's controls. Frantically, she touched buttons that resided across the dashboard until she found one that caused the thrusters to ignite from the rear. She looked towards the slowly exposing Exodus, but her attention was easily distracted further.

From the windshield came a shower of shards of glass that sprinkled upon her face and lap. A hand stretched from the roof of the vehicle into the newly opened front. She curled toward the back of her seat, attempting to get as far away as she could from the extending arm. To her left came another crash, this shattering louder than the first. Taupe skin filled her view from the side window. Timidly, she crawled back to the passenger's seat; however, no matter how hard she pulled, a pressure on her arm denied her progress. She looked back to find a grouping of five beige fingers piercing their way into her bicep. With a balled fist, she pounded the hand, but it was no use. Gradually, her momentum shifted in the opposite direction.

It was hard for Philips to navigate to a standing position seeing that his pain was nearly unbearable. He was assured that if he had not yet punctured a lung that his effort to stand was enough to send the sharp cartilage into the soft tissue. He wheezed as he dragged himself to the door of containment room. A handgun settled in one hand while he wrapped his torso with the other. The pistol was his only option considering he had generously wasted the rounds of his rifle on the being that rested behind him. Nonetheless, he knew he could make do with what he had as long he could make it to his destination, the nuclear room. He further struggled to the door and without much hesitation he opened it. The door parted and he raised his weapon, torso still guided. His first action was to check down the nearby corridor for life. Just as Rodriguez had experienced before, the halls were still, and aside from himself they were empty.

He was lost at first, but after wandering with a stumble he found a group of waypoints that held some familiarity. The pain was growing while the drugs had worn considerably. Again he stumbled, this time into a side wall. There he rested for a moment, attempting to breathe in sequence even though it had become almost impossible to do. Closing his eyes, he slowed his mind to somewhat of a thought-like beating pulse. Ambivalence orchestrated his thoughts. Torn between the thought of inevitable death and the future safety of all that he had known and loved, he trudged with great effort. In the back of his mind, he was approached by the very thing he had learned to distrust, not plead for his temporary safety but rather hope. The hope was for the guidance of some distant being. A safe and clear journey through the maze was all he needed. It was not a selfish, petty desire; however, he knew that no matter his intention it was something he could not do alone. The moment had come, where the very idea that had toyed with his life to that moment had become his last resort.

Philips reopened his eyes and recognized his position. Seeing that his pain had relentlessly attacked him, he had not noticed the time and distance that had past. He gathered himself, or whatever of himself that he could, and returned to his struggle. His hazy consciousness narrowed his vision to a tunnel-like surrounding. He was in terrible physical shape, for if he even came across one creature he was sure to concede the victory in favor of it. It was not a favorable reality, but his body could not sustain even the weakest of fights. Despite the thought, it would not be necessary. With a few turns, he had reached the final corridor he so desperately desired.

The corridor had placed him in front of nuclear room where he shuffled his feet to the key pad and opened the door. Alas, the door parted and the blue cylinder caressed his body with its echoing hue. He pinched his eyelids together, not from the brightness but from the pain. Ignoring it was hard, yet something else held more importance as he tucked his gun into his waistline. He felt his side, just below his hip and could feel the outline of an object. He gently traced the object with his fingertips. It was smooth against his conforming leg pant material. Vertically it was long, while horizontally it was slightly shorter. Physically, it was shaped to match a body of scale; however, spiritually it was fit to match what Philips truly desired. He reached deep into the pocket and pulled the object out. He stared at it for a moment as he pinched it between his index finger and thumb. The wood was not only smooth to the touch, but it smoothly aided the renewal of his faith. With his opposite hand, he removed his cross-less rosary, his wife's gift, and slid the beads through the looped side of object. Once the two were reunited, he returned it to his neck. He was at peace.

Philips pulled the gun from his waist-line and held it steadily pointed at the blue. He was not nervous and did not fear death. It was something that had to be done. Though it was odd to think so, he now realized that this was his purpose. All that he questioned and all that he lacked in faith had brought him to this moment. Through the sins of humanity he had found his path, he had found his answers. He was the protector, and he was to die to protect all that he loved and cared for. He was to destroy the evils that man had created; he was to be the savior of all that was good.

One pull of his finger would execute the deed as he readied himself. Suddenly, a sharp pain hit his body like a strike of lightning. Attempting to recognize its source, he realized it was not his injury. This pain came from an explosive echoing from his rear. He looked to his right pectoral and saw a red stain gradually promenade and expand across his uniform. With a gasp for air, he fell to his knees. Weakness spread through his body like a flood breaking a levy causing him to collapse his torso to the floor. There his face rested to the side against the cool floor, motionless. Vertically he was straight and long, while horizontally his arms stretch completely to their respected side. His body was covered in scars and behind him stood a man who did not express any sense of emotion. All that remained of the man was a blank face and an extended handgun. He lowered the handgun and studied the pool of red that filled the surrounding underneath Philips's lifeless body. Though the dead could not feel regret, this result was an event that could have been avoided. It was Philips's morality that prevented him from killing him while he had the chance. However, in the eyes of the conspirator this murder was just. What he did was necessary for the growth of his species, stopping at nothing to stop those who wanted to stop him. In the end, it was not the evil that had its victory, but its creator: a victory that gave him all he had ever desired, a victory that gave him his purpose—a victory that gave him perfection.

ON THE SEVENTH DAY

Exodus's grey sky characteristically faded into the planet's surface. The foggy, murkiness intrinsically moved through the terrain encompassing the planet with an ironic sense of comfort. The blanket stretched itself onto a figure standing atop a distant cliff. Slowly the figure raised its head revealing both its identity and face to the weatherly conditions.

The air was cool and crisp while the sky was grey from moisture. He could taste the dampness in the air as it seemed to ease its sensation over Him. The gentle caress of Exodus's atmosphere glazed His bare torso. He crossed His arms to hide the chill induced bumps across His body. The missions' uniform would have given Him the warmth His body craved, but it would have supported a connection to His past life. Accomplishment was the only warmth He needed as it flowed through his mind and body. There He stood on the cliff ledge looking for a vessel that was made nonexistent by the dense fog. All He could see was the newly populated planet that circulated below Him. Though He stood from a distance, He could see His perfection operating in masses to provide their livelihood. They communicated and moved amongst themselves with not only the efficiency to survive, but also to prosper.

This day was His day of reckoning, His day of new beginning. He had succeeded. His seven-day endeavor was complete, justifying the sacrifices that had ensued. With His goals reached, His ambition was somewhat curbed. He had now become content and realized His true self. No longer was He Nar. No longer was he even Narayan. He was now Narayana.